Sarah's Folly

Kathy Farinella

Printed in the United States of America

ISBN 1-57558-084-5

Acknowledgments

With special thanks to Laura Allis and Regina Hallmark for their generous help in the editing of *Sarah's Folly*. Also, with much appreciation, I dedicate this book to my husband, Rich, whose love, patience, and confidence have kept me going during the writing of it.

One

*W*hat have I done? Will I ever see him again? Will time forever refuse the moment to show him my true and deepest heart? Can I ever find contentment when my heart longs so desperately and continually to hold him just one more time?

I dream of him every night, and every morning I grasp at the memory of his image as it fades into the morning light. I dream of the feel of his curling hair around my fingers, of his dark serious eyes, and the trembling, passionate way he first pressed his perfect lips to mine. It was our wedding day.

John and I had strong convictions about physical intimacy and felt that the time and place to enjoy these pleasures was within the confines of the commitment of marriage. That's not to say that we didn't desire each other physically. On the contrary, it was like keeping two powerful magnets apart. But we arrived at our wedding day with the joy and satisfaction of knowing that we had kept ourselves exclusively for each other.

It was beyond wonderful to finally be able to explore every facet of our natures. With our physical convergence was a joining far greater, when his eyes met mine and our souls intertwined and bonded with the strength that only true love can provide. I knew in that moment that I would forever be his alone.

John opened up his heart to me as he never had with anyone before. This strong, commanding, and brave soldier became vulnerable to me. He let me tread on those secret and tender places of his heart with complete trust. I did the same for him. I felt that I knew him completely— every intricate part of his nature. That is why I was so astounded and dismayed when upon returning home, after leaving in an angry fury over an argument, I found him gone—clothes and all.

We had been married for two years, two wonderful years, the happiest of my life. At first I thought he was just angry and would come home in a few days. But the days turned into weeks and the weeks into months.

I was first angry, then bewildered, and finally afraid. For there was one commitment that John had made that was far greater than any other, even the one he had made with me. That was his commitment to God. He walked with God as a friend. He shined with His presence. He would never leave me, even if there were no love or tenderness between us, simply because he felt it wasn't right. That was the anchor between us that would hold us together throughout the roller coaster of life's emotions.

But he was gone, and no one knew where he was. I called all his friends and acquaintances and the Marine base where he was stationed, but every trail led to nothing.

If anyone could have found him it would seem that I could, for before these circumstances befell me, I was quickly becoming a competent reporter through tenacious investigating with the *Seattle Times*. It had been my dream of many years to be the very best reporter in all of the Northwest. I had already won several awards and felt I was finally on my way. This dream eclipsed all other desires, including marriage, family, and friends (to the dismay of my godly parents), and propelled me through college and quickly up the ladder of experience toward my goal. Nothing could stop me and even the still small voice of my God, urging me to surrender my will for His, would be reasoned away by my consuming ambition.

But for all of my success and shrewd investigating tactics, I could not unearth a trace of the only man who had possessed my heart so greatly that my career had to take second place.

I walked along, searching the streets where I had first met John. I'll never forget that day. He was so handsome in his dress uniform, his hat at his brow, his shiny sword at his waist. His platoon was marching along in perfect step to the strains of the Marine Corps Hymn in the Memorial Day Parade. Just as I was about to take a picture for a spread I was doing for the *Times*, our eyes met and held. Slowly then, I lowered my camera as I felt a charge of electricity surge through my body and blind me more than the most powerful cinematographic flash. I turned and watched him march away as I wondered at the intense attraction I felt toward this stranger.

He filled my thoughts all that night and the next day when I saw him seated at church, my heart almost burst with unreasonable longing to speak with him after the service. He glanced my way during the sermon and then again with recognition. Without a word being spoken I knew he felt the same as I. And if souls can reach out and touch another, ours met and held in unseen splendor, till at last we stood and began our short journey toward each other and a love that would rival any dream or goal that my heart could wish for.

But where was he now and what of the love that seemed so indestructible? Was it the argument? It seems so trivial now, looking back on it. I had had a hard day at work and had gotten home late. John tolerated my career because he knew how much it meant to me, but only tolerated. He longed to have our goals united and had even spoken in hushed tones of his desire to see his people reached for Christ, and a question if perhaps the Lord would, in fact, use him to accomplish this. John's father, who is deceased now, was American, but his mother was Arab, born and bred in Iraq. John's burden was for the Arab people, who are, like his own mother was, ensnared by Islam in every dimension of their lives. I dismissed these musings quickly, telling John of my goals again, to which he always listened with generous patience. So, he allowed me to continue on with one request—that I was always home to enjoy our evening meal together. I did this happily and made sure to come home in time to prepare something to eat that he would enjoy. That evening when I came home late, I was irritable and angry with a co-worker who had out-scooped me on a story that I had been working on for days. Feeling guilty for being late and irritated as well, caused me to re-act irrationally when John inquired as to where I had been. I flew off in a rampage about my own rights and reasons why he had no business requiring anything of me. The ar-gument escalated until I finally screamed I didn't love him anymore, and ran from the house to stay with my parents.

It was a foolish argument and I was clearly in the wrong. I lay all that night in my old room at my parent's home realizing how spoiled I was. I was an only child, born to a couple that had long given up the hope of enjoying parent-hood. From my earliest memories I was aware that I held the focus of their attention. Nothing did they deny me, ex-cept what they could not in good conscience allow. Basic discipline, such as respect, honesty, and accountability was unquestionably maintained, but beyond that the reins on my spirit were held loosely and I was free to do as I pleased and pursue my own desires. I knew that if I ever married, part of that freedom would have to be forfeited, and this knowledge kept me from any hasty commitments. I was fully aware of the curse women-kind inherited from Eve, and my submission that God would require. Not until I met John did I ever find a man who I thought was worthy of that humbling sacrifice; and, oh, how worthy of it he was! For he was integrity, godliness, and honor, all bound into one perfect physique. How I long to be held in those strong arms now! My only comfort is to find them in my dreams.

My dreams of John are like soap bubbles—I can peer into, cherish, and hold them in my hand for mere seconds before they burst and are gone. Within them I look for clues to find the moment John turned his heart from me. And though all circumstances make it evident that this happened at some point, I know somehow, with every instinct that reaches into a woman's soul, that it never did. It's not that I think John's love for me had evaporated that grieves me so terribly. It was the harsh words that came from my mouth the last time I saw his face. In this lies my torment. It was anger, uncontrolled, that caused me to say the untrue, cruel words that I did. It was anger that conceived the child of misery that stirs in my bowels. What rage could possess my judgment so greatly to cause me to deny the love I bore him? And does he think on those words now? Do they prevent his coming home to me?

Two

My dearest Sarah,

Please forgive my insensitivity toward your feelings and needs. Because I don't have the same make-up or wants, I easily forget to consider your desires. You are different and special—I'm so glad you are!

You are strong and spirited, and yet delicate and tender. You bring out aspects in my heart that would have remained forever buried without you. Through your softness I become strong and protective and yet, by the strength of your spirit I have confidence that you can weather the storms of life and face any challenge with courage that God may lay before us. Your bright and sparkling disposition transforms me into a miner with "gold fever." Seeing the jewels of your laughter drives me to dig deeper into your heart to win yet more of your sunshine. I can easily become lost in you. Just when I think I have fathomed your personality—you reveal corridors through which I have never explored. I don't know how you do it, but you continually keep me in suspense as to what you will reveal to me. I guess I can spend the rest of my life dedicated to discovering your being and never come close to exhausting who you are. I'll never fully understand you—and it's so new and exciting that way!

Your warmth attracts me home to you like a glowing fireplace on a cold and snowy night. Warmth is so difficult to define, whether it be of temperature or the warmth of shades of color, but it is always easily discerned by the physical and emotional sensation it generates. As to your warmth—I would be hard pressed to dissect and define it, but oh the flood of emotion your smile generates in me. I love you. I love being near you. You draw me to you as a boy is drawn to the aroma of a mother baking his favorite cookies. The warmth of your attention saturates me as a full afternoon sun satisfies a napping kitten. I know I must give you room to breathe, but my attraction to your warmth makes me desire to always be with you.

Sarah, right from the start I have loved you, and no doubt it was true love even as far back as the parade. But my love for you has continually grown to the intensity of this moment. It's as though back then I only thought I would love you, and today I love you experientially. You have proven to be much more than I thought you were. Our love diminished? On the contrary! Our love is proven and validated. It has passed the test of time with flying colors! Never have I ever regretted my choice of making you the object of my desire for my entire life. Not for one moment! I love you!

Why you continue to love me after so many mistakes is beyond me, but I thank God you do. Please keep loving me. I would die without your love. You are the princess that has made me a king. I don't deserve such fortune! But it's too late to withdraw now. I love you, I need you, and I can't exist without you! You are the lady of my dreams, the woman of my desire.

Always,

John

The letter was not a recent one. In fact, John had given it to me several months prior after a similar argument. I came across it by accident.

I read it over and over that evening as it tore at my heart and yet covered my wounds like a balm. It became more than that in the end. It became a catalyst that gave me the strength to try again to find the man who could utter such love and depth of feeling. He must still love me, he must! I said fiercely with new hope. Could such a love as this be destroyed in one night? Surely not!

The next morning I awoke with determination. I would go to the base once more to see what his military superiors had to say to me. They had to know something. Surely if he did not report for duty they would find out why. The last time I went there, everyone treated me like an annoying fly. The quicker they could shoo me out the door, the easier they could breathe. This time I would not be so easily dismissed.

I dressed in my business clothes and brought my tape recorder. These gave me confidence and I could use all I could muster at this point. I drove to the base and wondered again how I should proceed when I arrived. My biggest problem was that I didn't even know where to go, or who I should talk to. My work kept me so busy that I never took the time to enter into John's military life whether socially or otherwise. I deeply regretted that now.

The guard at the gate allowed me to pass and I proceeded to make my way to the main office complex. Upon entering I stood before a receptionist trying to explain my predicament. She listened patiently and then after a series of phone calls I was ushered into a waiting room on the second floor. This seemed promising, as it was farther than I had gotten before. I waited for an eternity, it seemed, when finally an older-looking gentleman entered the room. His uniform distinguished him as a high-ranking officer.

I took a deep breath, pushed record on my mini tape recorder and in my best newswoman tone, I began to ask probing questions. He immediately looked alarmed. I knew I had blown it when he turned and walked out of the door without answering a single question. I was ushered out as before and thought I could almost hear the door locking behind me.

Tears welled in my eyes and cascaded down my cheeks as I made my way to the car while fumbling for my keys. Then suddenly I heard a voice behind me.

"Excuse me, miss," said a young officer.

I turned around and looked at him while wiping my eyes.

"Aren't you John Morgan's wife?" he asked.

I caught my breath and looked at him intently. "Yes, I am," I answered hoarsely.

He stuck out his hand and said congenially, "I'm a friend of John's. I met you at your wedding a couple of years ago."

I didn't remember him, but asked anxiously, "Do you know where John is?"

He looked at me in surprise and then down at his feet. "Well, I don't . . . I mean," he stammered. "I gotta get going."

"You know, don't you?" I said grabbing his arm.

"Look, I could get in big trouble if I don't move on," he said. "I'm sorry I bothered you."

I looked at him pleadingly as my lips began to tremble and my eyes filled again with tears. "Please tell me," I cried. "I've not heard from him for almost two months. I've looked everywhere for him. I've tried everything!"

He stood there hesitating for a few minutes and finally turned to leave. Then he stopped and said, "Don't you ever read the news?" And with that he was gone.

I stood staring after him and then suddenly realized that he was telling me something.

Read the news, I thought. I write it! At least I did before this trouble came. When I didn't show up at work my boss called and I asked for a leave of absence. That was nearly two months ago now. Walt, my boss, had left numerous messages on my answering machine, to which I had failed to respond. I had been living in such a mire of misery that I had not even the emotional strength to deal with the reasonable demands of my employer. I cringed at the thought of facing him now.

I left the base and drove straight to the library. There I gathered the latest newspapers to see what was going on in the world. I was astounded. Every front page held the story that had rocked the world for the past month, yet somehow did not penetrate the emotional acropolis that formed my isolation. A group of fanatic Iraqi guerrillas had taken seven American hostages and were holding them at an old military prison camp just outside of Basra on the Iraq side of Shatt al Arab. Of the seven hostages, four were women—all political officers from the American embassy. The remaining three men were Marines, whose names, for some reason had been withheld. The guerrillas were demanding top-secret information and artillery from the American military that would make their small army as formidable as any, in exchange for the hostages. They gave us eight weeks to respond before they would begin to murder the hostages, one a day, beginning with the Marines. Our forces were deployed from every branch of service, surrounding the area with America's finest. The situation was tense with ultimatums, while countries rallied for support and politicians vied for the best solutions.

I looked up from the papers and felt a tremor of nerves shake my body. So troops were deployed . . . which naturally would include my husband, I mused. The thought crossed my mind with a shudder then that perhaps he was one of the hostages. I put that thought away quickly, as it was too frightening to consider.

My mind reeled with possibilities as the world around me faded like a pointless dream. My John was somewhere in harm's way without even the comfort of knowing his wife waits for him with love in her heart and her arms open wide. Or could he be grieving so heavily as I, causing him to give lesser care as to his safety? And if so, why didn't he write? Surely he knows me well enough to realize that my temper burns hot, but my love for him could not be so quickly extinguished.

I laid my head in my hands and let the tears escape from their swelling tide. If only I could have said good-bye. If only he'd left a note, no matter how brief, it would be such a solace to my heart. If only I had not left him that night. Regrets filled my heart in those moments until a small voice approached my reason with the words: Your separation is born of duty and honor, not of choice or love-loss.

Yes, yes, I thought, remembering the love letter I had recently uncovered. There has to be a reason for his silence aside from that awful argument. My heart groaned at the thought of his letter and the sweet words he penned and suddenly I cried to myself, "Give me one chance to reclaim those awful words I said! One day . . . one moment to hold him in my arms again. For this, I would trade my life."

I wiped my eyes then and made my resolve. I would reach him somehow, I determined. Some way, I would tell him of my love and never dying devotion!

Three

I decided to go home and write John a letter. I would mail it in care of his base and then pray that it would reach him.

It was one of those endless rainy Seattle nights, with low hovering clouds and a steady patter of drops that were rather comforting in their gentle rhythm. To this music of nature I lit a fire in the fireplace and sat down at my little table that overlooked the Puget Sound and began to write.

My dearest John,

For weeks now my heart has been grieved at your absence. I've learned one thing above everything else . . . that life is unbearable without you. My love for you is not a love that is moved by my anger, nor forgotten in your absence. It's not a love that flees at trouble or dies when provoked. I've found that it's a love that absorbs every emotional fiber, every breath, every movement that I make. I hear it in the rain. I feel it when the wind blows my hair. How I long for you! To touch your face, to hold you close. I dream of you every night, and though it's wonderful at first, at the last, it tears at my heart and I weep and try to put my thoughts of you aside. Yet, at every strain of music, every note of a melancholy symphony, every sound of thundering rain, you are there.

I am troubled by your absence, but much more by the remembrance of my ugliness toward you the last time I saw your face. How terrible I was and how hurt was your expression when I walked out the door. To think I said that I didn't love you anymore, consumes me with grief! To ponder if those words affect you now, is the bane of my existence.

Can you forgive me? Will you believe that my love is yours forever? When you lay down your head at night, it will be there beside you. When you are afraid, it will embrace and comfort you. It will be there in the dark of the night and in the pink glow of sunset. The cool evening breeze will carry it on its current and caress your face with its breath. The stars will tinkle it down in gentle kisses of light.

The Bible says that, "Many waters cannot quench love, neither can the floods drown it: if a man would give all the substance of his house for love, it would utterly be condemned." This is the kind of love I feel for you, my darling. It will never end, not in absence nor through years of monogamy. You are in my heart, your name is written there in the indelible stain of true love. May it be near to you while we are apart.

Your loving wife,
Sarah

I laid down my pen and read over the letter. Of all the pieces I had written for the paper, none held as much importance to me as this small declaration of my love. I wanted it to be perfect, and yet somehow I knew it could never say enough no matter how much I worked on it. I was never a poet, simply a journalist. It was not my custom to pour out my heart on paper, rather to just present the facts. Doing so now, however, was comforting to me somehow. It was as if I were speaking to John and some way he heard. Somehow through the miles that separated us, I was able to reach out to him with the tenderness my heart yearned to convey.

With the letter sealed and addressed, I laid down on my bed and let myself sink into the familiar image of the arms of my love.

The next morning I awoke feeling happier than I had in weeks. I decided that after I mailed my letter, I would head for the office and see if I could get back to work. It would be good for me to occupy myself with the absorbing details of my job. I had no idea how Walt would respond when I saw him. Perhaps he would take pity on me and let me slide back into my old position. On the other hand, it was conceivable that I had pushed him to his limit of patience and understanding.

After dressing with care, I picked up the worn leather case that held my laptop. It was laden with dust and I laughed at the sight. My computer was the one single item that I had used constantly for the past five years. Hardly a day went by when I had given it a rest, until now. Now I had to hold it up and blow off the dust, as if the idleness of my life had drifted in this form to lay on the symbol of my career.

It was thought provoking considering the life I had led. I had been determined to become a senior writer, to be placed on the executive committee who were assigned the best stories in the world. Relentlessly, I strove to out-scoop the veteran staff and had often stood in meetings to receive their scowling envy and reluctant admiration. What joy I found in this and how I exalted in my victories! Yet, it was all consumed by the loss of a love and the contender of grief whose strength is hidden to those of inexperience.

At these thoughts my father's sage words rang in my ears: "The more hurt you have in your life, the more capable you will be to help others." At what price comes this competence! I thought with wry humor. But for now I need to put this pain in my pocket and try to make some order in my life.

After dropping my letter off at the post office, I drove to the sprawling *Times* campus with a satisfied smile playing on my lips. Upon entering the building however, I felt my satisfaction drain into concern. What in the world would I say to Walt!

The elevator arrived on my floor and I walked, head up, into the familiar office center. Assuming some confidence I really didn't feel, I faced the raised eyebrows of secretaries and errand boys, who stopped their busy work to gaze at me as I headed for Walt's office.

"So, the vacation's over!" someone shouted as I rapped on his door. "Must be nice!"

"Come in!" Walt yelled in his familiar, annoyed voice.

I entered the room and found my boss discussing the day's business in earnest with his long-time secretary, Janet Copeland. He glanced my way and then again, this time with a look of surprise and a pause in his commanding instructions.

"That will be all for now, Janet," he said, dismissing her.

Janet walked over and whispered on her way out, "Good to see you, Sarah! Good luck!"

"So, what's up kid?" he asked, after she had left, in a fatherly tone that I was so relieved to hear. "Are you giving your notice?"

"My notice?" I asked confused.

"Yeah, I figured some other paper has sought you out and offered you that senior writer position you've been busting yourself to get. Or maybe a bigger salary!"

I was surprised, then flattered, and finally angry. "Don't you think I'd be a little more considerate than to leave you hanging with no word for two months, if that were the case!" I said with hands on my hips.

"That's just what you did!" he countered, facing me with the same stance.

I lowered my hands and sighed. "I know, Walt. It's inexcusable how I've neglected my responsibilities. But I would never consider another position without being level with you. You've been with me from the start and have given me my first leg up."

"Then what gives? Have you been sick?"

"No," I answered, looking at the floor. "It's personal problems."

"With John?"

"Yes . . . well, yes."

Walt looked at me in pity then. He, more than anyone, had witnessed the effect that John had had on me.

"Is it all worked out now?"

"Not exactly."

"What do you mean, 'not exactly'."

I looked up at Walt's concerned, yet exasperated face.

"John and I had a big fight," I said slowly. "I walked out and when I came back the next day he was gone. I haven't seen him since."

"Where did he go?"

"That's just it. He vanished. I haven't been able to find a trace of him."

"He hasn't called or written?" Walt asked in amazement.

"No."

"Isn't he in the military?"

"Yes."

"Well, he's in the Middle East with the rest of our boys, Sarah," Walt said, as if I were stupid.

"I assume that too, Walt. But his superiors act as though he doesn't exist."

Walt rubbed his hand across his baldhead. "Well, kid," he said after a pause, "I know you must have had a hard time. You really loved that guy."

"I still love him. And yes, it's been maddening."

"I wish you would have told me sooner."

"I couldn't face anyone."

"He could be on some military assignment, you know."

"Yes I know. . . . But he hasn't written," I said as a tear escaped my eye.

Walt came and placed a hand on my shoulder.

"What you need is to get back to the thing you love. The thing you do best."

"You mean reporting?" I asked, while wiping my nose.

"That's right, Sarah. You're the most promising young reporter I have," Walt said tenderly, in an unusual show of praise. "I was afraid I had lost you."

"Oh, come on, Walt. You've scores of young ambitious writers who could easily pick up where I left off."

"You're wrong kid. You have a gift. You can analyze the most complex situation in a moment and get right to the heart of the problem. Why, your articles say more in two paragraphs than most of my writing staff can produce in a whole page!"

I looked at Walt tenderly and smiled. I didn't buy his sentiments, but it was the kindest thing he'd ever said to me and quite out of character for him. I put my hand on his and said softly, "Thank you, Walt."

Four

*W*alt was right about my work. It was good to feel the keys under my fingers again, to watch a story develop, search for loose threads, and then to pounce on it at just the crucial moment. It kept my mind occupied and my thoughts away from my loss. It was quiet moments that would get the best of me, and so I would do my best to avoid them. As a result, I was getting a lot of work done. I took no rest, working late into every night. I became weary and tired often in those weeks after returning to work, but it was better than it had been before.

Walt looked concerned at times, but his eyes told me he understood. I saw also that he was happy with my work. It was fast-paced and on the edge. The way my whole life felt at this time. Walt favored me with the best assignments, to the chagrin of my co-workers. I could feel the brewing jealousy around me; and though in days past I could laugh in its face and count it a victory, it was now a burden that I felt was too emotionally taxing to deal with—and so, I did my best to ignore it.

The events in the Middle East were the main focus of everyone's attention at the *Times*. Though my assignments were only localized, I did my best to keep abreast of the situation, not only for work's sake, but for personal reasons as well. There were meetings with the department editors, who were under Walt's supervision, to discuss the situation almost daily. I attended every meeting as I had in the past, but this time I didn't stand around the edges of the group as an observer. I would take a seat at the large oval table and listen intently to everything that was said and sometimes make a comment. Of course, this was an affront to some and, because of it, I was becoming a little unpopular around the office. Having Walt's understanding was a comfort to me though and he was always ready to come to my defense.

The best part of my day would be coming home and checking my mail box. Hope would surge through me each time I put my key in the box and each time my hope would be lost in the impersonal communications of junk mail and bills.

This day I arrived home and placed my briefcase on the floor before my mailbox, as was my custom and fumbled with my keys to find the right one for the box. After dropping the keys, picking them up, and searching through them again, I was finally able to fit the right key into the box, but not without a little frustration. When I opened the small door, I caught my breath as I saw the familiar envelope lying on top of the rest of the mail. It was the letter I had sent to John. I picked it up and read the large red words stamped across the front of it: "Return to Sender."

It was obvious by the postmark that the letter had never left the Marine base. I began to fume with anger. How could they! I thought. Did they really expect me to risk losing my husband in such a dangerous situation, without even communicating with him! This was more than any war had ever demanded. Or maybe he's not there at all, I thought suddenly. Maybe he's dead!

I shook my head to lose that thought. No, I wouldn't believe that. He's alive somewhere needing me as I need him!

Inside, I sat on the sofa, turning the letter around in my hands. I'm back at square one, I thought, still not reaching him with my love and apologies. The thought occurred to me then to look up on the computer the island base where our ground forces were stationed in the Persian Gulf. There is a web site that I had used often for work, where I could send a message to a satellite that would take a video picture of any place in the world that I would request. It was highly unlikely that even if John were there that I would get a chance to see him this way. The picture would only be of the outside of the complex, as the satellite camera could not penetrate walls, but at least it was something.

I sat at my computer and punched in the address and the area where the base was located. I had to search then a while to find the proper location, but finally was rewarded by a hazy video picture of large white tents, buildings, and machinery that almost faded into the sandy landscape.

There were few visible signs of life from this vantage. Most of our troops were more than likely working underneath the shade of a tent or inside a building to avoid the obvious heat that I could almost see in the air. Some stood guard around the complex, but these were all but covered in their brown camouflaged uniforms.

After a few moments of searching the picture, I breathed a heavy sigh and leaned back in my chair. This wasn't getting me anywhere. I thought then, with a shudder, to try and find the prison camp in Basra. The names of the Marines that were being held prisoners there had still not been released. I kept telling myself that the odds of John being among them were very slim, but it was still a nagging fear.

With trembling hands, I worked the computer to bring me my desired picture and at last it came. A group of old concrete buildings, surrounded with barbed wire, tanks, jeeps, and men with machine guns, filled the screen. With a start then, I saw the large figure of the back of a man, whose stance and commanding presence filled the small fenced yard where he stood with some other men. I held my breath as I zoomed in to get a closer look at this man whose build and broad back were the image of my John's.

Only a brief moment did I get to study this picture before it was jerked away, with only a small printed message left in its place which read: "This web site has been confiscated by the United States Marines."

Like everything else in my life, I thought with anger as I kicked the desk with my foot.

My anger was soon replaced with worry though, as I considered the picture I had just seen. Was it John standing there in that small dismal yard? The way that the man stood and the height of his stature were so like my husband's.

That night I tossed and turned as I dreamed of my love. I dreamt that I had found John and was just a few feet behind him, calling out his name. There was something holding me so that I couldn't go any farther, and so I just kept calling and crying so that he would turn around. He never did and I awoke choking with sobs and with his name on my lips.

"Please God," I prayed out loud when I was fully awake, "let me see him just once more. Just one more time let me look into those dark eyes and tell him of my love."

Five

At work the next day the office was buzzing. Walt had decided it was time to send a reporter to the Middle East. The natural choice was, of course, our international affairs reporter, Ivan Vanhorn, but something inside of me gave way to a hope that perhaps Walt would allow me to take the assignment. It was really a highly presumptuous idea for me to even think that I could vie for the opportunity, having never even covered a story outside of the U.S., not to mention one of such importance, but as soon as the assignment was revealed, I knew I had to do it. True, it was for personal reason's that I was motivated, but it was the story of a lifetime and one that I knew I could make good on. Not only that, Ivan Vanhorn was the most boring writer I had ever read in my life. He could take the most exciting happening and make it sound like a monotonous lecture.

If I was allowed to go, I could search for John in the process of covering the story! Only a press badge could bring me into his vicinity. It was more than I could have thought possible or even had considered before, but after the return of my letter yesterday and a night passed in desperate dreams, I was ready to fight for this chance with all that I had.

A staff meeting was called and as I entered the room the excitement of anticipation sent a boost of energy to my trembling body. All were seated and Walt began to give the details of the assignment and what he expected to gain from the overseas excursion.

"I want to know exactly what's going on over there," he said forcefully. "Something tells me that we're missing a critical point of information. Things just don't add up. The government over there denies any involvement with the guerrillas, yet will not aid us in any way."

"It's been puzzling to me also, Walt," added Megan Miller, the religious editor. "I expected the guerrillas to call this another 'holy war,' but to hear it confirmed in a positive light from the political officers in the area, really surprised me."

"Yes, there's a contradiction of words and actions from several different aspects of leadership in the country," Walt continued. "Even in those who assert that they are appalled at the fanatics' actions, one can see an obvious admiration. I need someone to go and sort through the maze of demands and accusations and try to make some sense out of all of this."

"I find it odd myself," Ivan Vanhorn interjected, "that the names of our Marines have been withheld by our own government. We've seen no videos of beaten, bloody soldiers, or even the frightened women that they've retained. This has got to be a first in modern conflicts."

"It could be that the guerrillas don't have the equipment for such scare tactics," Walt said. "This is said to be an independent attack from a remote nomadic sect."

"Well, one thing's for sure," said another reporter with emphasis, "you couldn't pay me enough to go over there!"

Walt looked sternly at the young reporter. "That's our job in the newspaper business, to go where the trouble is and find the answers. It's what the public expects and they have that right. We need people with courage and brains to send out into these situations and if you lack either, you've taken up the wrong profession."

The group looked sober at Walt's rebuke.

"Well, my bags are all but packed," Ivan said confidently.

Walt looked at him with creased brow. I could almost

read his thoughts. Ivan may have the courage, but not all the brains that he would like.

"I'll go," I blurted out.

Everyone looked at me in surprise.

"That's ridiculous," Ivan said.

Walt looked at me with an expression that mingled exasperation, understanding, and pride. I could see his mind was turning.

"You're not really considering sending her, Walt!" Ivan demanded.

"I don't know . . . She is my best writer."

"What!" he shouted, insulted.

Walt eyeballed him and said again, "She's my best writer."

Ivan had to back down on that point, but quickly retorted with, "But she's a woman!"

I was offended at that and raised my chin and chest.

"You know how those people feel about women. It would be far too dangerous!"

"You do have a point there," Walt conceded.

"Walt," I said in defense, "the press always stands beyond prejudicial boundaries. When was the last time a member of the press was harmed because of color, sex, or creed? It doesn't happen because we are neutral in these matters."

"That may be true in most situations," Ivan countered, "but we are obviously not dealing with reasonable people. These people not only don't respect women, they hate Americans! And look at you, you'd stick out like a sore thumb. You're American apple pie with that blond hair and blue eyes!"

"Don't you think you're going a little overboard with your stereotyping!" I asked Ivan accusingly.

"All right, you two," Walt refereed.

I turned then to Walt and whispered pleadingly: "Please let me go. I'll . . . I'll quit if I don't get this assignment!"

"Are you threatening me, Sarah?" Walt asked in reserved anger.

"Oh, Walt, don't look at me that way. I have to do this. And I'll do you a good job!"

Walt studied the intensity of my face.

"All right then, Sarah," he said after a moment of contemplation. "I'll give you a chance."

"Oh, thank you!"

Ivan hit his fist on the table. "This is too much! You've favored her on every good assignment in the area. Now you're letting her move in on my domain!"

"Hold it now, Ivan," Walt said, raising his hand. "She's not going on this assignment alone."

I looked quickly at Walt and thought, Please don't say you're sending Ivan with me.

"You're going with her, Ivan."

I closed my eyes in reluctant compliance.

Ivan said nothing for a moment.

"That's more like it, but I'm in charge."

"That's fine," Walt said, "but I want this report to be written by both of you. Do you understand?"

Ivan and I looked at each other. There couldn't have been another person that I clashed with as terribly as Ivan. We saw things as differently as any two people could. But, if the truth be known, the story was not my first concern and if anything, even working with this man, could bring me nearer to John, I would do it.

"All right, Ivan," I said in a pride-wrenching show of humility, "you're in charge and we'll pull this off together."

He looked at me in surprise and then mumbled reluctantly, "All right."

After some instruction the meeting was adjourned. As we got up to leave, Walt took me aside.

"I'm giving you this chance, Sarah and I want a thorough investigation."

"You'll get it!"

"I know you want to look for your husband and that's okay, as long as it doesn't interfere with your work."

"Thanks, Walt, for understanding."

"Good luck, kid."

Six

After a whirlwind of activity, Ivan and I were seated on a plane heading for Tel Aviv. We would arrive there, travel to Jerusalem, and then take a military transport to the island base of military operations in the Persian Gulf. Walt had given us a week to gather information and expected us back then without delay.

I could hardly believe I was on my way! With each mile crossed, my heart seemed to groan hungrily at the thought of getting even that much closer to John. If only Ivan wasn't seated next to me, I could have thoroughly enjoyed this new experience. He was constantly making remarks as to his superior experience in international affairs and writing skills and told numerous success stories to back up his claim. I had never heard such blatant bragging.

Not only did he brag, but he made a point to subtly put me down at every opportunity. I realized that only someone who was very insecure would act in this way, but still I was unable to muster up the sympathy that I should have offered. When he began to bait me with questions that would give his desired response, I began to become annoyed. I couldn't stand to be manipulated.

"Have you ever camped in the desert?" he asked.

"No," I answered.

"It's not a pleasant experience."

"It's what our military is doing," I said.

"Yes, they're out there spitting sand and trying to sleep in that unbearable heat."

"They knew the job was dangerous when they took it,"

I answered with a cliché.

"I hope they weighed the risk. That would be more than I could say for some."

"Meaning?"

"Meaning, I don't think you know what you're getting into."

"I have a vague idea."

"There will be no room for primping and keeping yourself dolled up as usual."

"Oh, I don't know if I could endure that," I said sarcastically.

"You do know that we are supposed to be staying on the military compound, don't you?" he asked.

"Yes."

"It's not going to be comfortable."

"I don't expect it will be."

"You know there's a really nice hotel that I stayed at once in Tel Aviv," he said as his voice took on a soothing quality. "It was full of local color and charm. And the food! It was out of this world!"

"Really."

"Yes, I was thinking that maybe you'd like to stay there and not have to go on to the Persian Gulf. I could go ahead, gather information, and meet you back there to compile our story."

"You mean, your story," I said, becoming a little irritated. "I would have nothing to contribute in those circumstances."

"Sure you would. You could get a feel for the area and help describe the climate."

"Look here, Ivan," I said turning to face him. "I didn't come all this way to find a few local descriptive adjectives or take some kind of exotic vacation. I came to write the biggest story, thus far, of my career. And I'll make any sacrifice that it takes to write that story!"

"You're as impossible to work with as I thought you

would be."

"Perhaps we should work separately then."

"Maybe we should. I've always been a maverick, you know. I don't know if I would want my articles tainted with your sensationalistic journalism," he said, with stabbing insult.

"Then it's settled," I said, ignoring his cutting statement. "You write your story and I'll write mine. We'll let Walt decide what he wants to print."

"You know you'll never get the real story," he sneered. "Women aren't even supposed to leave their homes in that part of the world without a written permission slip from their husbands."

"I'll manage."

"You know, it may do you good to live in a culture like that for a while. Where women learn to keep their place."

That statement was the last straw for me. I got up and found another seat. One thing was for certain I determined then, I would out-scoop Ivan Vanhorn if it was the last thing I ever did!

After landing in the modern city of Tel Aviv, we took a cab to a small promontory called Jaffa which jutted out into the Mediterranean Sea. The historic Jaffa was once the ancient city of Joppa, where Jonah fled from God's presence to catch a ship to Tarshish, and where Peter raised the disciple Tabitha from the dead by the power of God.

We arrived in Jaffa late in the day, just as the sun made its long shadows across the land and touched the sea with a rosy hue. It was a lovely evening and I wished that I was not so tired, so that I could enjoy the new sights and sounds of this unique and aged city. We would have to leave early in the morning to catch a bus to Jerusalem. From there we would fly to the island base on a military transport plane. From what I had gathered, it would be a long and tiresome day of travel. I had been advised to get a good night's sleep.

When we arrived at the hotel however, I was overcome by a nostalgic sense of reminiscence of my favorite old movie, *Casablanca*. The hotel bore a striking architectural resemblance of the portrayed "Rick's Cafe Americain," with its large arched columns and lush green palms. Even the music that was playing was performed by a small, smiling black man who effortlessly rattled the keys of an old rolling upright piano.

Ivan noticed my dreamy face and asked as we were checking in, "You're sure you don't want to stay here for the week?"

It would be nice, I thought, if John were here. "No. I came to work," I answered firmly. "But, this is a great hotel."

That evening I sat on the terrace in my room, which overlooked the Mediterranean Sea, until late into the night. I couldn't help myself. The moon was large and full, and the air was sweetly scented by orange blossoms that filled a small tree nearby. I let myself dream of my John and a night spent here in the contentment of his embrace. It was surely just my imagination, but it was as if in that moment that our hearts united in combined focus and I could almost feel his large rough hands around my face. I closed my eyes and leaned into those shadowy fingers and kissed them as they drifted away.

Seven

The next day we were up early to catch our bus to Jerusalem. It was a lovely morning and I was excited about the day's adventure.

As the bus traveled down the historic highway from Tel Aviv to Jerusalem, I was enthralled by the landscape and the bus driver's comments as he expounded on points of interest along the way. The Bible stories of my youth came alive as I could almost see David, the shepherd boy, tending his sheep on those same rolling hills, and our Lord Jesus feeding the five thousand.

In my exuberance I exclaimed to Ivan, sitting next to me, "It's just how I imagined it would be!"

"What is?" he asked puzzled.

"The area. It's just how the Bible describes it!"

"The Bible!"

"Yes . . ." I stammered and then realized that Ivan did not know that I was a Christian. What an indictment that was on my conscience! What was worse was that it may have been better that he didn't know, as I had been such a poor testimony with my quick temper and aggressive disposition. Had I forgotten so easily my responsibility to be a witness for Christ? I could recall a time at youth camp, when I was a teen, when the Lord drew me near; and my deepest desire was to show someone else the way to Him. But Ivan Vanhorn of all people! I was still mad at him from the previous day and I had not tried to hide my feelings. But perhaps, with the Lord's help, I could make amends.

"Yes, Ivan. I grew up on Bible stories. I'm a Christian,"

I said gently.

"Really," he answered in mocking tone. "I never would have thought."

I grimaced at his words.

"There are places in this vicinity that you would be better off keeping that a secret," Ivan whispered. "There's a lot of tension in the air. I could sense that at the airport. Armed guards everywhere and cloaked Muslims bearing attitudes that were just as alarming."

"Ivan, don't you realize that Muslims in this area assume that most all Americans are Christians, just as most all Arabs are Muslim?"

"Yes," he answered uncomfortably. "I guess you're right."

"They don't realize that a Christian is one who makes a conscious choice to accept the Lord Jesus as their Savior and not simply a follower of Christ by location of birth. . . . I think the Muslims' disturbed attitudes stem mostly from the old complaint of being driven out of this area in 1948, when God restored this land to the nation of Israel as was His promise and a significant fulfilled prophecy."

"Oh?"

"Yes. Many Arabs still live in poverty in refugee camps near Jericho and have since the restoration. Their only hope (in their mind), is to reclaim the area in another 'holy war,' and have brought up their children ever since with this in mind. They still retain several Muslim holy sites in this region, such as the Dome of the Rock, which has prophetical significance as the Bible declares that the Jewish Temple will exist on that same site and, knowing this, the Arabs are not unduly protective. Of course, they cannot fight the true and living God and will be someday overcome, as not one of the prophecies of the Bible has ever failed."

Ivan looked at me thoughtfully. "It seems like they would just give it up, knowing they can't win," he said.

"Oh no!" I said with a chuckle, "They would never admit that they can't win. The rivalry between the Arabs and the Jews goes back thousands of years to, some say, Sarah and Hagar, the mothers of both nations. When God promised Abraham that through his seed he would make a great nation, and Sarah his wife, through her unbelief, gave her servant Hagar to Abraham to bear a child for him; deeming herself too old to conceive."

"I can't imagine a woman doing that today!" Ivan chuckled.

"It wasn't uncommon then, but certainly just as unwise. Abraham was a wise man, but somehow Sarah was able to persuade her husband to help God work out the fulfillment of the promise. When he did this, he willingly disregarded God's power and resorted to human contrivance. From that time of Sarah's folly, problems multiplied as mutual dislike and jealously set the two women at odds and preluded an inheritance of hate for their offspring, the Jews and the Arabs. Of course, God did give Abraham a son through Sarah at the appointed time and Isaac would be the father of a great nation and through him all the nations would be blessed as it was through his line that God would send his own Son, the Messiah, the Lord Jesus. There was so much of God's plan for the redemption of the world that began with Isaac that Abraham just couldn't see. He was limited by his lack of faith and it is still a lack of faith that inhibits us all from following God's will as we should."

"You talk as though the whole course of history was already laid out by God before it ever happened," Ivan said incredibly.

"It was, Ivan. Not only the past, but our future as well. If you're a student of the Scripture you can see that many of the major events of history were foretold and happened as the Bible said and that we can know full well what our future will be. There is no guesswork about it. Only a fool disregards such obvious information."

"So what happened to Hagar?" Ivan asked.

"Well, Sarah was harsh to her. So harsh that she fled from her into the wilderness. God came to her there and comforted her and promised her that He would bless her son and multiply his descendants. He also promised that he would be 'a wild man; his hand will be against every man, and every man's hand against him; and he shall dwell in the presence of all his brethren.' "

Ivan chuckled. "Well, those promises were obviously fulfilled. Certainly, no one can tame the Arabs and they're always fighting with everyone!"

"Yes, it has been said that when Arabs are not at war with an enemy, they will always be at war with one another. They are probably the least liked and most misunderstood of nations. They have also been taken advantage of by foreign exploiters who recognize this weakness."

"What about the promise that 'he shall dwell in the presence of all his brethren?' "

"It's interesting to note the fulfillment of this promise. Did you know that the Arab people are among the best examples of biblical nomadic tribal life available today? They have never been uprooted from their habitat and therefore have been able to preserve their cultural traits and conserve more of their traditional peculiarities."

"So," Ivan asked with a puzzled expression, "was Hagar happy with these promises?"

"Apparently so. The Bible says that she was so overcome by God's presence that she called the name of the Lord that spake unto her; 'Thou God seest me.' I think she thought that her son would never live to become a man, and that she was just a servant that God could never care for. She had seen the relationship that God had had with Abraham and heard how He had come to him and told him, 'Fear not Abram: I am thy shield, and thy exceeding great reward.' That God would come to her as well was probably beyond her fondest hopes or more than she would dare to ever dream."

"What did she do after that?"

"She went back to her mistress and submitted herself to her as God had told her to."

"That must have been difficult."

"I'm sure it was, but it's obvious by the Scripture that Abraham cared for Ishmael. That must have been a comfort to Hagar."

"And galling to Sarah."

"Well, Sarah had a special position in God's plan that set her apart from all other women. Sure, it must have been galling to have Abraham love her maid's son, but knowing the promises toward her own son could not help but give her a sense of justice. Besides, the problems with Hagar and Ishmael were of her own making. If you think about it, the world as we know it would be quite different had that one woman not made that one bad choice."

"In what way would it be different?"

"Muhammad, who wrote the Qur'an and founded Islam, claimed that his people were descendants of Ishmael. Whether they were or not we don't know, but Muhammad was an Arab nevertheless and through the Arab people this religion has been born. No other religion in the world has fought as tenaciously to overcome God's plan and turn the hearts of men away from His Son, the Lord Jesus Christ, and the salvation He offers."

"Surely, if God is who you say He is, He knew this ahead of time. Why would He allow it?"

"I cannot begin to understand all of God's plan at this time in history, but it can be observed that God has used this people to bring about part of his prophetical plan throughout the history of the world; and I believe will use them in the future."

"In what way do you think?"

"Well, it's only my conjecture, but the next prophetical event that will take place, according to the Bible, is the catching away of the Lord's bride or His church. We call it the Rapture, when those people who have placed their faith in the Lord Jesus will be caught up to be with the Lord. Those unsaved, or unbelievers who are left behind, will face a seven-year period of first peace and then tribulation."

"I've heard of that."

"Well, during this time the Bible teaches that the prince of 'Rosh, Meshech and Tubal' will move southward in an attempt to conquer Israel. Rosh is modern Russia who will join with allies including Persia, which is called Iran today; Togarmah, which is modern Turkey; and Gomer, which is still a common name in East Germany. The one thing that these countries already have in common is an increasing sympathy with Islam. Islam is now, actually, the fastest growing religion in the world. They have already gained momentum in Afghanistan; and the former Soviet republics of Turkmenistan, Uzbekistan, and Tajikistan are all Muslim states. To the west of Afghanistan is Islamic Iran, while Pakistan lies to the south and east. There are several theories as to the motivation of the coming attack on Israel, but as I said, it is all conjecture, the Bible does not give a motive. But it seems to me that with the hate and revenge against Israel that Muslims have been instilling in their children for years, and the increasing march of that religion across the face of this part of the world, that a combined effort of, what they would consider, the ultimate victory of defeating Israel in a 'holy war' in the name of Islam, would be the logical conclusion."

"Where would that put America?"

"With Israel, I suppose. We have traditionally been their ally, which is a wise stance as God promised that He would bless those who blessed Israel, and there is no doubt that America has been blessed. But, who knows what the future will bring. Men of faith have not ruled our country as of late and in fact, there will be few left with faith in America after the Rapture."

Ivan looked thoughtful for a moment. "You know a lot

about the Bible and really believe this 'plan' of God's, don't you?"

"I've always enjoyed learning and have been in church all my life. My pastor is a good teacher, and yes, I do believe that God has a plan for us and that it will all come to pass."

"I'm surprised that you didn't become some kind of preacher or missionary, instead of a reporter."

"Women can't be preachers, Ivan. I suppose I could have gone into some kind of Christian service."

"Why didn't you?"

"I don't know."

I was silent after that as I thought about Ivan's question. The truth was I never considered if God had other plans for my life besides the ones that I had designed. I never even asked Him. I guess I was afraid He would tell me.

"Look," Ivan said then. "We're coming up on Jerusalem."

I leaned forward and looked intently out of the window. The city was large and as modern as any, which was not my expectation. I asked the bus driver about the ancient sites and famed wall with gates that was supposed to surround the city.

"Oh, you're talking of the old city of Jerusalem which is just southwest of here."

"Oh," I said with disappointment, "I was hoping to get to see a few sites along the way."

We arrived at the bus station at ten a.m. and were supposed to catch another bus at two that would take us to an American military compound nearby. From there we would fly to the Persian Gulf.

"We have a few hours to kill," Ivan said when we got off the bus. "How about finding a good place to eat?"

I looked around at all the parked buses, with roaring engines and placards which told of their various destinations. Then I saw it. A bus with "Old City Tour" displayed on its placard. "Look, Ivan!" I said with excitement, while grabbing his sleeve. "There's a tour bus going to the Old City! Maybe we could have enough time to see a few historic sites before we leave. I've always wanted to visit Mount Calvary!"

"I don't know . . . It would be a big mess if we missed our transport."

"Let's find out how long the tour is!" I said, as I ran to the bus.

The bus driver, who thankfully spoke English, told me that the tour was short and would be back at one-thirty. They were just ready to depart, however, and if I were going I had to get on the bus now.

"Ivan!" I shouted, while waving my hand for him to come. "Come on!"

Ivan hurried over and asked, "Are you sure this bus will be back on time?"

"Yes, yes," I said, while pulling him aboard.

The bus took off before he could reconsider, and we had to stumble along to find a seat. Ivan threw our bags on the ledge above and sat down with a chuckle.

"You sure know how to get what you want," he said.

"I'm sorry, Ivan. I just couldn't pass up this opportunity."

"Well, you've got it now," he said as the bus began to roll. "What makes this place so important anyway?"

I looked at Ivan in surprise. "You're not serious are you? Surely you know the significance of Jerusalem."

Ivan shifted uncomfortably in his seat. I could see that I had unwittingly stabbed at his ego. Before he could retaliate I quickly retrieved the insult.

"Unless you mean its significance to me as a Christian."

"Of course that's what I mean. You don't think someone of my world knowledge would be ignorant of the history and culture of such a prominent international player as

Israel?" He asked as he smoothed his ruffled feathers. "I was merely referring to your own biased viewpoint."

"Yes, of course," I answered, smiling inwardly at his quick response to climb on my ego to protect his own. And I would allow him to climb in the name of Christ and for the sake of his soul, which price I had to value above my pride. Actually we had made great strides today in our relationship, having had our first civil conversation. And Ivan had listened to my viewpoint with patience and respect. I had to give him that. It would do no good to revert back to the old banter and lose the ground I had gained in making him a friend and giving him a witness.

"And Ivan," I continued humbly, "I appreciate your interest in my point of view."

Ivan looked a little surprised and then warmed to the compliment. "Only a fool reporter would not listen to every angle. It's what gives me the edge when I compile my information in cases of complex perceptions. How do you think I got where I am!"

"Yes . . . well."

"Go on then," he said condescendingly. "Tell me why Jerusalem is so significant to you as a Christian."

"All right," I answered slowly. "We have to go back to the story of Moses. You know that story, of course?" I asked carefully, holding my breath to see if I had offended him again.

"Of course I know that story," he answered with a roll of his eyes. "Doesn't everyone? Moses takes the children of Israel out of Egypt after many signs and wonders, they wander in the wilderness for forty years and then go to the Promised Land."

"That's right, Ivan. I'm impressed."

"Thank you."

"Well, when they got to the Promised Land the Bible says that 'all these kings (that inhabited the land) and their land did Joshua take at one time, because the LORD God of

Israel fought for Israel.' After having defeated the inhabitants, God divided the land. The land on which we now travel, this city of Jerusalem, was given to the tribe of Judah. Through the lineage of the tribe of Judah, God promised to send the Messiah, which He did and which was our Lord Jesus Christ. This land then, is in essence, the very inheritance of the Son of God from His human perspective. I think perhaps that that is the very beginning of the importance that God has placed on this land. It is more than the home of the Jews or the right of their ancestry, it's the place of inheritance that they share with none else but the Lord Jesus Himself."

"Hmm . . ." Ivan mused.

"Since that time," I continued, "Jerusalem has been the focal point of God and the place where He chose to place His name."

"It's so small and insignificant!" interjected Ivan. "As a matter of fact, Israel as a whole is no bigger than the whole state of New Jersey."

"It is amazing, isn't it. But God always favored the weak and lowly. And if you notice, Israel is always the center of world concern and media attention."

"That's true enough."

"The Bible says that someday Jerusalem will be the center of worship for the whole world and the place we call heaven that God is preparing for those who love Him, God has called the new Jerusalem; holy Jerusalem that will descend out of heaven from God. You should hear how the book of the Revelation describes that city, as it were a great square gem; actually made up of every precious stone imaginable, with gold for its foundation and pearls for gates and from within shines the very light of God, and that city will descend from heaven for all the world to see! Can you imagine such a sight? All of man's cunning and insightful city planning could never rival this one!"

Ivan stared at me.

I glanced at him and said, "But now I'm getting ahead of myself. That's in the future. The past also holds a great wealth of historical prophetical events, that if examined could do nothing else but convince one of the authenticity of the Word of God and of God Himself. More than anything else, Jerusalem is the place where the Lord Jesus died for our sins and that single event was the pinnacle of all time for all of mankind. It was the day when God the Father redeemed fallen man with the ultimate price of His Son's blood and proved forever His love toward us. All men, believers or not, number their days from that time and it is the day that God will point to for all eternity."

"There's a lot to this 'plan of God' as you say, that concerns this area then," Ivan said after studying my face for a moment. "It will make this short tour all the more interesting."

Eight

The bus driver began to speak then as he drove the noisy bus through the busy city and then across the ancient vicinity of old Jerusalem. The first place he brought us to was a great castle area called the Citadel. It was one of the oldest and most famed sites in the city and sat high on a hill.

"The massive masonry you see before you," the bus driver/tour guide spoke in his thick Israeli accent, "was known as the Tower of David in times past. We call it the Citadel at present and it now holds the Museum of the History of Jerusalem. The interior of the Citadel contains remains that date back to many different periods in history and is probably the site of the Praetorium, where Jesus was condemned to death."

We were let off the bus then and were given a thirty-minute period of time to look around. As we entered the ancient courtyard, I was struck with a surreal feeling of stepping back in time and seeing the same things that our Lord Jesus had seen at the time of His interrogation before the cross. How primitive it all must have seemed to Him who created all the laws of architecture and knew what the extent of man's construction abilities would be. What must have been His thoughts when man, in all his crude finery, stood before the judge of all the earth—this one who was wisdom personified—and sought to accuse. What else could He have done but stand in cognizant silence.

Our time was quickly spent reviewing Jerusalem's history inside the museum, which contained, in fact, the same historical accounts and stories that I had been taught throughout my life in Sunday school. I pointed out to Ivan the persons and object lessons throughout this Old Testament time line that were "types of Christ" that all pointed to the coming Messiah and did my best to give Ivan an overall sense of God's plan that brought us up to the period called the "Age of Grace" in which we now live. There were times when my Bible knowledge failed, but it seemed the Lord was with me and guided my words when my mind was at a loss. The time passed quickly and Ivan was kind to give me his full attention and show a fair amount of interest.

From there we boarded the bus and made our way to the Temple Mount which stood at the edge of the city just inside the Eastern Gate. Beyond the gate was the Mount of Olives from which our Lord ascended to heaven after His resurrection and to which Zechariah prophesied that He would return. As we stepped off the bus, I stopped and stood gazing at this sight, as memories of sermons reflecting the significance of that mount filled my thoughts. Ivan roused my attention as the group moved forward into the massive park setting that encompassed the Temple Mount.

Though the large temple of Islam called the Dome of the Rock dominated the area, our Israeli guide directed our attention and our steps to the Jewish sacred place of the Wailing Wall. He began then to solemnly give the history of the wall and spoke with such feeling that I wondered if such emotion could be rehearsed.

"After the destruction of the Temple by the Roman emperor Titus in 70 A.D.," he began, "this wall, which was actually not a part of the Temple itself but possibly one of the four supporting walls built by King Herod to enlarge the Temple platform, or perhaps part of the wall that surrounded the outer forecourt, nevertheless became a symbol to the Jews of the Temple and the place where they would come to mourn the loss of it. For centuries the city authorities prohibited the Jews from setting foot on this holy mountain and their longing to once again have that privilege cannot be fully understood outside of their culture. The loss of the Temple and the Jews' captivity was so tragic that the Jewish calendar marks the day of destruction of the Temple in 70 A.D.—the ninth of Ab—as the Day of Lamentations. Generations of Jews have visited the wall to lament their fate, and for this reason it has come to be known as the 'Wall of Lamentation,' or the 'Wailing Wall.' The traditional belief of Judaism is that the Temple cannot be rebuilt until the Messiah comes. Only after the reunification of Jerusalem in 1967—nineteen years after the founding of the modern state of Israel—did the Jews finally take possession of the wall. The sight of hundreds of exhausted Israeli soldiers crying at the wall, having entered this holy site after years of exclusion, will never be erased from the memory of those who were present that day. Since that historic event, thousands of Jews from all over the world have come to pray unhindered at the wall."

When the tour guide finished his epilogue, I turned to Ivan and spoke in hushed tones, "Did you know that Jesus prophesied of the destruction of the Temple?"

"No, I didn't," he answered.

"Yes, and He said that not one stone would be left upon another. As a matter of fact when Titus destroyed the Temple and burned it with fire, he realized that the gold that overlaid the magnificent structure was melting and seeping down between the stones. When the fire died, he ordered his soldiers to take the Temple apart, stone by stone, in order to retrieve all of the gold."

"And so, he fulfilled the prophecy in doing so," Ivan concluded. "Very interesting."

The group turned then and began to walk toward the Dome of the Rock as the guide, once again, began to speak.

"When the Muslims appropriated the Temple Mount area and built the Dome of the Rock and Aqsa Mosque upon it in the seventh century," he said with distaste, "they banned Jews from the site. We long for the day when this mount will once again contain only the Temple of the Jews."

"Whoa!" Ivan whispered. "Talk about World War Three!"

"You're exactly right," I agreed.

We stopped then to stand before the eight-sided, gold-domed temple of the Muslims as our guide continued his lesson in history.

"Many revere this place as the site of the rock on Mount Moriah where Abraham attempted to sacrifice his son, Isaac, in obedience to God. As we know, God only wished to see the depth of Abraham's faith and love and when Abraham demonstrated this, God provided a ram to sacrifice in place of Isaac. This same rock is also believed to have once been used as a threshing floor, the threshing floor of Araunah. For those of you who are familiar with the Bible story of the threshing floor of Araunah, you will know that it is the place where God halted the punishment that was meted out to David for numbering the people against His will. To commemorate this event, David purchased the rock from its previous owner and built an altar there, where he sacrificed in repentance. Later, David desired to build a Temple for the Lord on this site, but was disallowed by the Lord because his hands were bloody from the many wars he had fought. So, David prepared the materials for his son Solomon to build the Temple after he was gone."

The guide had spoken these words with such reverence that when his tone changed suddenly to one of hatred, it pulled the attention of not only the tour group, but the natives who were mingling about the area.

"Though history proves otherwise, the Muslims believe that this same rock, aforementioned, is the place where their prophet Mohammed last placed his foot before his departure from this earth," he spat. "Therefore, they have made this shrine to enclose that rock."

"He sure doesn't hide his animosity."

"No, he doesn't," I said. "As a matter of fact, you can see it on the faces of some of the Israelis in the area, as well as some of the Muslims."

"It seems to me that some of these Muslims are showing their disgust more toward this tour group than anyone else."

"If you notice, they are sending those angry signals to those women in our group who were wearing skimpy clothing. Did you notice that they even required some of them to put on robes that they provided before they could enter this area."

"I think you're right."

"Yes, I've read that they often feel assaulted by the inconsiderate dress of the Western women entering this area, wearing shorts and immodest clothing. They are deeply offended by this constantly, while most Westerners haven't a clue that they are offending."

"Why should they be so offended by what the women are wearing?"

"Because Islam teaches an extreme spectrum of modesty for women. In Iran, which is an Islamic state, women are covered from head to toe in black and this manner of dress is enforced by the law. Women improperly dressed face harsh consequences. Women tourists who uncover their bodies and walk around in Muslim 'holy places' dressed in this way, are disrespecting Islam. The sad thing is, in the Muslim mind, Christian and Western ideology are one and the same. The depravity that is witnessed by the world by means of Hollywood, Muslims believe, is a byproduct of Christianity. They don't want this kind of sensual and fleshly influence in their society. But the truth is, as we should know, that the philosophy of mainstream America and the movie industry are in direct opposition to what the Bible teaches. Christians in America also protect their children from this sort of degradation, and a woman who is a true disciple of Christ will follow the biblical instruction to adorn herself in modest apparel."

"That explains why you're wearing that long dress and scarf. I thought it was strange, being that the weather is so warm."

"Actually, I try to always dress modestly. I want to please the Lord. But today I took extra precautions because I knew that I might be on Islamic turf."

"I wonder how long this will be Islamic turf," Ivan pondered out loud.

"Somehow I don't believe it will be long."

"Because of the tension in the air?"

"No. Because of the fig tree budding."

"The what?"

"The fig tree budding is an allegorical reference given in the Bible for the prophesied time of Israel's restoration in 1948. The prophecy also said that further end-time prophetical developments would occur within that generation. A generation, according to the Bible, is anywhere from thirty-three years to one hundred and twenty. But at the latest, if my eschatology is correct, we are living within that generation."

"You mean the generation that will see the . . . what did you call it? The Rapture?"

"Yes, Ivan. That, among other things such as the Temple being rebuilt here."

"All part of 'the plan' you've been talking about all day, huh?" Ivan asked with a chuckle.

"Yes."

"I see."

"Do you really, Ivan?" I asked earnestly.

"I see that you believe that this Temple Mount area will not forever be Islamic turf."

"Do you not see how immutable and amazing God's promises are?"

"According to everything I've seen and heard today, yes, they appear pretty amazing."

"Ivan," I said touching his arm. "The most amazing of all is the price that was paid for the redemption of our souls."

Before I could continue with that thought, the bus driver hailed us to return to the bus. Ivan turned to follow his instruction.

"Come on, Sarah," Ivan called. "Our last stop is Mount Calvary. You can preach at me some more there."

We boarded the bus and made our short trip to Calvary in mere minutes. During the drive, our tour guide/driver expounded on the outlying areas that we would not have time to visit. How I would have loved to have been able to stop at the Garden of Gethsemane that lay at the foot of the Mount of Olives.

The driver also explained that there were, in fact, two sites in the city that claimed to be the true "Place of the Skull" or "Golgotha." One was now the home of the "Church of the Holy Sepulchre," and the other was known as "Gordon's Calvary."

"We will visit my preference, 'Gordon's Calvary,' " he went on to say. "Because of its peaceful atmosphere and pleasant ambiance, many are inclined to view Gordon's Calvary and the Garden Tomb as authentic, finding it more amenable to devotion than the dark and noisy interior of the Church of the Holy Sepulchre."

When we arrived at the site, my heart was pounding with emotion. Be it the true site or no, it was certainly a vivid portrayal of that most holy mount.

Following our guide out to the place where our Lord was supposed to have hung on the cross, I felt a lump rising in my throat and swallowed hard to prevent the tears that were threatening to burst. How I longed to be here alone with my Lord and commune with only Him on this historic mount. As the guide began to speak and hold the attention of the group, I took the opportunity to slip away, just a little farther to be alone.

Seeing Mount Calvary affected me more than I could

have imagined. It was just a rocky hill overlooking the valley, but in my mind's eye I could see my Lord there, dying for my sins.

The wind howled across the plains then and I could see that thundering day, when the sky turned black and rocks and hills gave way as God's wrath for man's sin shook all of creation. What agony must have been the Son's when the Father turned His face and Jesus cried: "My God, my God, why hast thou forsaken me?"

It was for me, my heart cried at the thought. Never, since I have known the Lord, has He ever forsaken me. Not in the depths of my rebellion, or after the most wicked sin. When I come to Him with repentance, He never turns His back. He's always ready to receive me in full knowledge of my condition. Yet Jesus, His only begotten Son, because of the sight and the stench to God of the sin that He took on that day, was forsaken when He called out to the Father.

I could not think of greater despair, than to call His name and not be able to see His face or find His presence. The severing of this most vital link must have been the most painful of all the reparations that He bore that day. And this He did willingly for me. Me, Sarah Morgan, who would give more thought to herself than to her God. A weak and foolish woman in whom rests only a spark of concern for the things of the Savior. I felt ashamed to stand in that holy place.

I dropped to my knees then while tears cascaded down my face. I don't know what Ivan must have thought, but I didn't care. My focus was on my Savior and my desire was to express to Him the thankfulness I felt in my heart.

I blessed His name and felt my heart burst with the wonder of His love. And at that moment, a change took place within me. I saw the world and my place in it, in a new light. I was His disciple and that would forevermore be my first priority.

Ivan came up and placed a hand on my shoulder. "Are

you all right?" he asked.

"Yes."

"This is where Jesus died on the cross, huh?"

"Yes, Ivan. This is where, some say, He came to die for our sins. Yours and mine."

Ivan fell silent.

"Remember the story I told you of the sacrifice lamb? Of the plan of God and the foreshadowing of the ultimate sacrifice that He would make for mankind?

"Yes, Sarah."

"It was here that God demonstrated His love by giving His Son, the Lord Jesus Christ, as a 'blood sacrifice' for the sin of mankind, to redeem us unto Himself. He is called the Lamb of God. It was the single most important event that has ever taken place. Ivan, do you understand the significance of it?"

"I'm not sure I do."

"Let me make it clear," I said standing to my feet and looking him seriously in the eye.

"God our Creator set down laws, His laws for us to live by. Over time it became obvious, because of our sinful natures, that we would never be able to totally keep those laws. But God's holiness demanded recompense for our sin. It was determined by God from the beginning, that He would pay the price Himself one day and redeem us through the Son of God, the Lord Jesus Christ. As an illustration of that coming event, the Lord commanded that the children of Israel would take a spotless lamb and sacrifice it as an offering to God, for a substitute of themselves to make reconciliation for their sin."

"I understand, Sarah."

"When the Lord Jesus died on the cross, it was the ultimate sacrifice and show of God's love. The only request He makes of us is that we repent of the sin in our hearts and that we receive this great gift. The gift of salvation."

Ivan looked away uncomfortably.

"Ivan, do you want to receive that gift?"

"I . . . I don't know Sarah. What do you mean by 'repent'?"

"Only that you confess yourself a sinner, turn away from your sin, making the Lord Jesus in fact, Lord of your life."

"Sarah . . . I don't know if I'm ready for such a commitment."

"But if you only knew how wonderful He is! How much it means to have His presence in your life . . . " I said and then hesitated for loss of words.

Ivan gazed past me toward the valley.

"Maybe someday I will," he said finally and then turned and walked away.

Nine

We made it back to the bus terminal with just fifteen minutes to spare. I was famished and knew Ivan must be also. Without a word to Ivan, I ran quickly to a vender who was selling local foods to the people mingling about the terminal. There was so much offered that I was unfamiliar with. I chose two bottles of water for Ivan and me, some fruit, crackers, and dried figs that looked appetizing. It wasn't much of a lunch for a grown man, but at least it would sustain us until we could find something more filling.

"There you are," Ivan said as I approached him with food laden arms.

"I was hungry and knew you must be too," I said. "And I couldn't let you starve on my account."

"What do you have?" Ivan asked, looking in the bags.

"Not much, I'm afraid."

"Well, we'd better find our bus before we miss it," Ivan said, his eyes scanning the rows of rumbling buses.

After finding our military bus and climbing aboard with the rest of the press corps, we settled down to eat our meager meal.

"Sorry about this, Ivan," I said. "If it had been left to you we would have eaten well instead of sightseeing."

"Oh, no," he answered generously. "It was worth the trade. I learned a lot."

I smiled then as hope sprung up in my heart. Perhaps a seed had been planted after all. I would make it a matter of prayer that, hopefully, that seed would germinate, take root, and that Ivan might be saved.

After arriving at the American military compound, Ivan and I and the rest of the press corps, were ushered directly to an awaiting transport plane. There were twelve of us altogether. I was the only woman.

The crew onboard the plane were very hospitable and I wondered at the cooperation that seemed unusually apparent to me. After a while, an officer stood and began to introduce himself.

"I'd like to greet you all on behalf of the U.S. Armed Forces and welcome each member of the press here today to the Middle East. I am Captain Gerald Montgomery and I am here to brief you on what you can expect and what we expect of you. As you know, this is a highly volatile situation and we need your professional discernment to rise above any need to find an exclusive story."

Ivan and I looked at each other with raised eyebrows.

"Of course, we can't tell you what to write, but realizing that the safety of our troops is at stake and moreover, the success of the operation itself, we ask for your full cooperation as we lend to you the information for you to give to the public that will least jeopardize the mission."

"Isn't this a violation of freedom of the press?" I whispered to Ivan.

"Hold it now, rookie," Ivan said, in warning tone. "We are talking war here and the safety of those hostages."

I nodded my head and thought of John.

"From the onset of this situation," the captain continued, "our commanders in charge decided that a working relationship with the press would be in the best interest of everyone involved. I realize that the information released has been sketchy and somewhat mysterious, but trust me, we deemed this approach to be essential."

I looked out of the window with a creased brow. I understood the point, but what this man was saying went against everything I had been taught about journalism.

"How can the military buy the press?" one reporter asked accusingly.

"We buy it with the lives of those hostages!" the captain retorted hotly.

The group was silent as Captain Montgomery visibly regained his composure.

"I realize that you are all in competition as you represent your respective newspapers and magazines," he said, "but I'm asking you to lay those natural motives aside for the greater good of our country."

"When we arrive on the island," he continued, switching gears, "there will be a press conference held for you with General Pierce, who is, as you know, the commander in charge of this crisis. He will give you the information that he sees fit and explain the highly sensitive aspects of our maneuvers. He will answer minimal questions and we ask that you refrain from baiting the general with questions that will produce only frustration and cause him to appear awkward in the face of the public."

"And finally, we hope you find the accommodations we have arranged for you adequate and if we can assist you in any way, please feel free to ask." With that, Captain Montgomery sat down and a low murmuring replaced his controversial speech.

When we arrived at the small military island in the Persian Gulf, we were again greeted cordially and then led to an awaiting buffet dinner, of which Ivan and I were very grateful. The meal consisted of a variety of chilled salads, fruits, and fish, which compensated the sweltering humidity that could be felt even within the air-conditioned building.

After the meal, we were immediately directed to a small room containing a podium and a few dozen chairs. It was here that we would have our press conference and await further instructions concerning our stay.

I was beside myself with anticipation, hoping with all I

had that John was somewhere on this island and that perhaps I would see him mingling about the soldiers who were present from every branch of service. Ivan saw my excitement as my eyes scanned every corner within the reach of my vision, mistaking it for a reporter's Utopia.

Ivan chuckled. "Your first press conference, aye?"

"No."

"Oh, I thought perhaps it was."

"No, it's not the first, but it is the first of such international importance."

"I bet you're excited," he said.

"Yes," I said with hesitation, realizing my mind wasn't even focused on this momentous event in the history of my career. My love for John had overcome that aspect of my life two years ago and it continued to pale in the face of my desperate longing to convey that sentiment once again.

I took out my notepad and readied myself for the conference. I had to put my attention here. I owed that much to Walt.

General Pierce was then announced and entered the room amidst our applause. He was a stocky man in his mid-fifties, with a no-nonsense attitude. He quickly dismissed the applause, seeming embarrassed by it, and got right down to the business at hand.

"Members of the press," he spoke loudly, "you have been welcomed here today, in what we feel is an open show of cooperation. We hope that cooperation will be returned. What we have been facing in these months is an inexcusable act of abduction and extortion from a small nomadic tribe of Arabs called 'San'ie.' The San'ie have neither the support of the government in Iraq or the military. What they do have and what we find disturbing, is the support of Muslim-owned newspapers and a seemingly large percent of the general public. Here, they are admired and touted as heroes. Though no one expects the San'ies to achieve their ultimate objectives in obtaining top secret information and artillery in exchange for the hostages, we fear the growing sympathy for their cause among the area's population, could result in the weakening of that nation's resolve to stay aloof from the crisis. This would mean a small skirmish expanding into a major conflict. We must avoid this at all cost. For this reason, our plan of attack has been designed to incur the least amount of media attention and to be as low-key in this part of the world as we can make it."

"Of course," he continued, "if it came to blows, our military could quickly extinguish not only the entire San'ie tribe, but cripple this nation in a matter of days. Our presence on this island alone guarantees that nothing happens within a thousand-kilometer circle around us without our permission. That radius extends far inland by increasing our operating tempo, including the vicinity of Basra and southern portions of Iraq. If need be, attack missiles can be launched from both the Red Sea and the Persian Gulf from our nine cruisers, five destroyers, two battleships, and two nuclear-powered attack submarines that are in the vicinity. Our Navy and Marine Corp aviators are on standby to quickly eliminate Iraqi air defenses and to command and control capabilities. We own the skies, the sea, and the earth with our technology."

He continued on in nothing short of bragging of our country's technological achievements and I had to admit, I caught some of that pride and patriotism that he so vigorously displayed. It brought an amount of comfort to me concerning John, until his proud banter was sobered when he concluded in what we may receive in losses.

"Of course, it is conceivable that in the end, we could lose those Marines and women who are being held hostage. The people we are dealing with seem to know no bounds of reason and appear willing to murder the hostages at any provocation. It is a very delicate situation and demands our wisdom and patience above the need for retaliation."

I sat staring at the general when he was finished, while reporters around me wrote furiously and hands rose, while questions were put forth.

"What exactly is the 'plan of attack' that you referred to?" one man asked as General Pierce granted him the floor.

"Our plan of attack, which we have dubbed 'Silent Storm,' is of such a clandestine nature, that our exposure of it to the press would mean its defeat."

"Is operation 'Silent Storm' already in progress?" another reporter asked.

"Phase one of operation 'Silent Storm' has been launched with surprising success," the general answered cautiously, "but we are withholding phase two until our government's Crisis Intervention Team confirms that they have made every attempt to negotiate a peaceful settlement with the San'ie."

"Is a peaceful settlement a possibility?"

"From all indications," the general answered sadly, "I'm afraid it doesn't look promising. You see, the San'ie are not professionals. You could say that they could be likened to a Los Angeles inner city gang—simple, uneducated, and proud—trying to take on a world power who has every military resource available. They have been raised to hate Americans and live to one day triumph over us. This bias has made them unreasonable. They are like a stubborn child, refusing to come in out of the street. With the Muslim-owned newspapers portraying them as brave patriots, their confidence has grown and has made them reckless with pride."

"How soon do you expect to engage phase two?" the same reporter asked.

"Of course, since this is a covert operation, I am not at liberty to answer that question," the general answered. "But we are at twenty-two days before the promised executions begin and we will give the San'ie every possibility for reasonable negotiations without endangering the lives of our people."

With that, General Pierce stepped back away from the podium and Captain Montgomery advanced and said, "That will be all the questions the general will receive at present. At this time, you will be given an itinerary for the week and escorted to your rooms. We thank you for your attention and consideration on the behalf of the United States Armed Forces."

I looked over to Ivan. He sat scribbling notes on a pad and then glanced up at me.

"You getting this, Sarah?" he asked as I sat still and thoughtful.

"I'm thinking."

The itinerary was then passed out and I looked it over. Almost every free moment of our time here was arranged for us to be viewing our country's fighter jets, touring the military compound, and listening to lectures on the principles of national security and composure in times of threat. It could not have been clearer that our reports were being molded and channeled by the military. Somehow, though I understood the reasoning behind it, it was an offense to me.

"Ivan," I whispered. "Did you read this?"

"Yes."

"Doesn't it strike you as an obvious attempt to thwart one of our most basic freedoms—the freedom of the press?"

Ivan gathered his papers and prepared to stand. "I think it will only make our job easier and I think if you don't get off it, you're going to be booted out of here before you can quote the first amendment!"

The group rose then as an officer instructed us to follow him to our respective assigned lodgings. As we walked down the corridor he explained that the men in our group would be bunking together in a dorm situation, while myself, being the only woman, had been assigned private quarters.

Ivan turned and looked at me with a wry grin. "You

always land on top, don't you?"

My room was small, with a steel bed, white walls, and gray tiled floor. There was a small desk with a glaring florescent desk lamp on top and a metal folding chair before it. The word "sterile" came to mind, but I shrugged my shoulders and was thankful that at least it was private.

It could have been much worse. I had envisioned sleeping in a canvas tent, while mosquitoes swarmed around my head and the heat and humidity stole my breath. Yes, I was thankful for this small, air-conditioned room.

I took my clothes off, turned out the light, and got into bed. I was so tired. Visions of the day's experiences danced through my mind and it seemed I had lived a lifetime in one day. And then I thought of John. He could be so near, laying his head upon his pillow now and relaxing his large muscular frame. At the thought of his body, I yearned for the physical fulfillment that we had enjoyed and had been denied for so long. But there is so much more to John, I thought then, than his outward shell. Though I am thankful for it, it affects my love and esteem for him only as much as a jewelry box affects the value of the diamond inside. The man he is within is the diamond, the Crown Jewel, the Hope Diamond to me. And when someday his mighty strength fails and his frame is worn and frail, his worth to me will remain unchanged. He is indeed much more than a body or face. He is the consummate of honor and virtue and the better part of my heart.

Ten

The next few days Ivan and I and the rest of the press, spent fulfilling the prearranged program of the military. We listened to lectures, toured secure shelters, and learned everything imaginable about the technological capabilities of our war machines and aircraft. I thought wryly that I could fly a jet myself by the time this was all over. And all the while I looked for John.

Too soon, it seemed, we had been over every inch of the small island and had looked over the shoulder of every technician. There was no sign of John. I began to carry a picture of him in my pocket and ask the soldiers secretly, when the opportunity arose, if they knew or had seen him. It was as if he didn't exist, and I began to feel frustrated by the futility of the whole venture.

Not only was I frustrated by my lack of success in finding my husband, the whole arrangement by the military regarding the press began to really bug me. I felt as if I were being manipulated, and nothing else produced more of a stiff back in me than when my hand was seemingly forced.

It all came to a head one afternoon, as the combination of these agitations were topped off by an arrogant officers' insult to my profession.

He was giving a lecture on military procedures (to which I had had my fill) and it was evident from the start that the man was somewhat lacking in people skills.

From the minute he opened his mouth, he lost his crowd. He began with, "Today I have been assigned the tedious task of instructing the peanut gallery . . ."

I folded my arms and whispered to Ivan, "Does he really mean us?"

"Apparently so," Ivan whispered back through the side of his mouth.

The officer continued. "It seems to me that you've been given enough information to write a book, if you've been able to understand half of what we've been spoon feeding you. Of course, I realize that reporters have little need for methodological details of any happening, only what they can sensationalize and sell . . ."

Before I could think better of it, my temperamental disposition had gotten the best of me and I was standing to my feet and telling the officer just what I thought of his rude statements and the military's coercive practices.

"I've had just about enough of this," I said loudly with my hands on my hips. The officer looked startled.

"Do you think we want what you've been 'spoon feeding' us? I've got news for you, we knew you had enough ammunition here to blow up the world before we got here," I said sarcastically. "If any insightful or interesting story can be written out of the repetitious rations that have been dished up to us here, it'll take a genius to compose it."

Laughter from my comrades drifted around me.

"What we want to know is, what do those nationals think about two million guns pointed toward their homes and the possibility of World War Three erupting around them? And do they really think a small fanatic group of warmongers have the right to put them in this kind of jeopardy? I believe the press can do a world of good by simply hearing the opinions of everyone involved—the military and government, as well as the civilians."

"We are here, miss," began the officer, "to help and protect you in the best way we . . ."

"You could help us infinitely more by getting us off this isolated island and out where the action is."

"That is not permissible. The danger would be far too great, particularly for a woman such as . . ."

"And where do you get off calling us the 'peanut gallery'?" I interrupted again angrily. "I suppose sitting around in your officers' lounge playing 'Battleship,' or planning another two hundred alternate plans of attack, would be a better use of your time!"

The officer's face turned red at that and I could see that he was fumbling for a retort. Apparently, nothing came to mind, for after a moment, he gathered his notes and stormed out of the room.

All was silent as I stood there looking after the man.

"Bravo!" said a fellow journalist finally. "Served him right!"

Ivan stood then and began to pick up his things. "You had your say, rookie," he said. "But I fear you'll pay for it."

"Pay for it, how?"

"Pay for it by being shipped out of here on your ear. You'd better start packing."

It seemed Ivan was right, for it wasn't ten minutes later that a young soldier entered the room with a message for me.

"Ms. Morgan."

"Mrs."

"Mrs. Morgan, General Pierce would like to see you in his office at eighteen hundred hours.

"That's six o'clock?"

"Yes, ma'am."

The soldier left the room and I put my face in my hand.

"Don't fret too much, Sarah." Ivan said in sympathy. "We've got everything we need and everything were gonna get here anyway. I'm ready to go home myself."

I appreciated the consolatory words, but the reality was, if I had to leave now, I would be leaving with infinitely less than what I had come after. It would be a harsh reprisal for my thoughtless and caustic repartee.

After leaving the conference room, I made my way outside to sit on the beach. The sun was just going down and the sky and sea were ablaze with color.

I couldn't see the land to the north, the land called Persia in days gone by, but I knew it was there. And there, perhaps, was also my husband. A prisoner in a filthy prison camp. Hadn't I thought that I saw him by satellite?

How could I go now, after coming all this way, without knowing? If only I could get across this water. I would go to my mother-in-law. She had moved back to Iraq just after John and I were married. With John's father dead, and the marriage of her only child, she had gone back to her people. She said her elderly mother needed her. Surely she would welcome me, and she lived near Basra. I had the address in my laptop. Possibilities began to rumble in my head.

But this is madness, my common sense told me. There are boats all around me, but every one well guarded and made for war. Besides that, this island base is aware of every fish that swims by. No one comes or leaves this place without their full knowledge and permission.

I fell back on the sandy beach and moaned. This is impossible, I thought. I picked up some sand and let it run through my fingers. It reminded me of an hourglass and the fact that I had to face General Pierce in only two hours. How I would like to avoid his summons! What would he say to me?

I was thinking on this when I heard suddenly a small outboard engine coming along the beach. Raising up on my elbows, I watched a weathered dingy sail past me and then to land on the beach only a few feet from where I lay. Out of it jumped a dark little man, his head bound in a turban, wearing a short robe, with jeans underneath. He seemed out of place among the uniform-clad soldiers of the island and I watched him curiously.

With practiced hands he lifted a dolly, placed it under

one of six wooden barrels that sat in his boat, and swung both over the side and onto the sand. As he began to roll it across the beach, as best he could, an idea came to my mind and I jumped up and ran to speak with him.

"Excuse me," I called loudly, as I approached him.

He stopped and turned to look at me.

"What do you have there in that barrel?" I asked, hoping he could speak English.

He looked me over and then asked indignantly, "Who are you?"

"Oh, good," I answered with relief, "you speak English! My name is Sarah Morgan. I am a reporter for the *Seattle Times*. I'm here by permission of the military."

He looked satisfied with that. "Rice," he said then. "Rice and beans I deliver."

With that he turned and continued to push the barrel slowly up the beach toward the back of the mess hall. I fell into step beside him and continued our conversation.

"What do you get paid to deliver these goods?"

He grinned widely and said with pride: "Twenty American dollars!"

"And where do you come from?"

"Kuwait."

Suddenly, there appeared two armed guards from inside the building and greeted the little man. "Hello, Ibn! Whatcha got there today?"

"Just rice," he answered, rolling the 'r'.

"Ahh . . . why don'tcha bring us something good now and then, like some more of those Turkish delights you brought a few weeks ago?" the soldier asked with feigned disappointment.

"I only bring what cook says," Ibn answered.

They let him pass then with a smile and a shared laugh between them. I followed, trying to look as innocent as possible.

I watched Ibn deliver the barrel from a distance. After

a word to the cook, he left the one he brought, and picked up another that was obviously empty. I walked back outside, down to his boat, and waited for him to return.

As he heaved the empty barrel back into the boat, and proceeded to haul another out, I whispered his name. He looked at me oddly.

"Ibn," I said again. "How would you like to make a hundred dollars?"

"How?"

I looked around to see if we were being watched. "Take me back to Kuwait with you."

"Bah!" he said. "I would go to jail forever."

"Five hundred dollars."

"It's impossible. We'd never get off the beach."

"I could hide in the barrel."

"No," he said as he shoved the dolly and load over the side.

I leaned toward him and whispered then; "One thousand American dollars." He paused at that and I knew I had him.

He stared hard at the ground and then looked me in the eye. "You have cash?"

"Yes."

"Meet me in the kitchen storeroom in fifteen minutes," he said and then turned and began to push the barrel.

With excitement I could hardly contain, I made my way quickly to my quarters. With haste, I grabbed my small bag and shoved inside only a few necessities along with my wallet that contained the two thousand dollars I had brought with me in cash. I hesitated at my laptop and then decided it was a must. Without allowing myself a moment to think about what I was doing, I forged ahead, and pushed any fear aside.

The kitchen storeroom was located just down the hall from my room and I slipped inside without the notice of anyone. The room was dark and quiet and I moved to the far wall where I would be the least conspicuous should anyone other than Ibn enter. After only a few minutes, he came in hauling an empty barrel and hurried over to where I was.

"Quickly," he whispered. "Get in!"

After handing my few belongings to Ibn, I climbed in the barrel. He gave them back to me once I was inside and told me to crunch down as small as possible. He then placed a roughly woven sack over me.

"I'm going to cover you with some rice," he said. "You must lay very still."

He poured the rice over my back then and I felt it fall through the sides and against my arms. I had to protect my breathing space and I did this the best I could by arranging my things around a little crack in the barrel. It would have to suffice.

"We go now," Ibn said, and I felt the barrel being lifted and rolled along.

We were doing fine till we got outside. It was there that anxiety gripped my heart and I thought my own trembling would give us away. The two soldiers that had spoken to Ibn before had approached and were questioning him about the rice in the barrel.

"What's this Ibn?" one of them asked. "You're supposed to be delivering rice, not taking it."

"Well, you see," Ibn answered in a fearful voice, "cook say he don't want this long grain rice left from last time. He say he want only Thai Jasmine rice to make sticky rice. You see?"

"What are you talking about," the officer answered. "Rice is rice."

"No," the other guard said then. "You're wrong, Brad. There are several different types of rice. Thai rice does make the best 'sticky rice.' My wife makes it all the time along with this curry chicken that's out of this world!"

The soldier went on about his wife's cooking and soon

70

I felt the barrel lift and begin to roll as the men's voices faded in the background. Shortly, I heard the waves crashing, and felt the dolly shoved under the barrel and it along with my person being swung high into the air. At last, we were in the boat!

It wasn't until the motor had started and I felt the small craft skidding across the waves, that I let out a sigh of relief.

"Do you think I can come out now?" I yelled to Ibn above the roar of the engine.

"Not yet," Ibn yelled back. "Wait a little longer."

I tried to relax in my little space. I had been so overcome with fear that I hadn't realized how uncomfortable this was. It also hit me then that I would soon be missed when I didn't show up for my appointment with General Pierce. Of course, Ibn wasn't aware of my summons and the trouble that could be brought on him so quickly. It hadn't occurred to me until now, or perhaps I would not have endangered him this way. That's what I get for not taking time to think, I thought wryly.

"Can we go any faster?" I yelled then.

"She's at full throttle!" Ibn answered.

I closed my eyes and thought it was about time to pray and then felt suddenly ashamed to approach the Lord. I had recklessly forged my way without taking time to inquire at my God. How could I expect Him to clean up the mess I made, when only a few days ago I had promised to make His business my first priority.

But I had to pray. Only God could help me now. "Oh Lord, I'm not sure what I've done. But please . . . bring me safely to my husband."

Before long, we had arrived on the beach of Kuwait. Ibn secured the boat, and then proceeded to once again haul the barrel that I crouched in over the side. He rolled it over behind a small building and then began to remove the rice covered sack that concealed me.

"Here we are," he said.

I stood up slowly, easing my cramped muscles out a little at a time. How good it felt to drink in the night air. It had grown dark and I thought that though it was a good thing for my escape, it did cause me a little apprehension.

Ibn helped me out of the barrel and then said, "My one thousand dollars, please."

"Oh, yes, of course," I answered and then fumbled through my bag for my little wallet.

Ibn stood with his hand extended.

"Here you are. One thousand dollars," I said as I placed ten one hundred dollar bills in his hand.

Ibn said, "Thank you," and then turned to leave.

"Wait a minute!" I called frantically. "You can't leave me here. I need to get to Basra!"

"You asked me to bring you to Kuwait," Ibn said, "not Basra."

"Please, I need your help," I begged. "I'd never get there on my own."

"I could not do this. We could not cross the border."

"There must be a way."

"Too risky," he answered, shaking his head.

"How far is it to Basra?" I asked.

"One hour and fifteen minute drive."

"Well, that's not too far at all!"

Ibn rubbed his short beard in contemplation. "Tell you what," he said finally. "I take you to the border . . ."

"Oh thank you!"

" . . . for one thousand American dollars."

"What?!"

"I could leave you here."

"But I can't do it!" I said, knowing it would clean me out.

"Okay . . . seven hundred."

"Five."

"You could bring me lots of trouble."

72

"You would have to haul rice and beans for a long time to make fifteen hundred dollars."

Ibn smiled, revealing his lack of front teeth. "All right, Missy. You win."

I clapped my hands together.

"You wait right here and I will be back."

Ibn left and I waited. It seemed a long wait and I thought how foolish I was to put so much trust in a man I didn't know. What if he got scared and never came back, or what if the military caught up with him before he had a chance to return. Or worse, what if he took me somewhere, only to rob and take advantage of me or even kill me. My thoughts began to run wild then and I began to shiver.

And then I heard footsteps. They were coming toward me and I crouched down to hide behind the barrel.

"Missy!"

It was Ibn. I stood and called, "I'm here."

"Put this on," he said and handed me a black chador to cover my head and a long black robe.

"Follow me," he ordered after I had donned the garment.

He led me, not far, to a little square car that was riddled with rust and covered in dust. We got in and he took off.

It was too dark to see much, but I could tell that the landscape consisted mostly of sand and tumbleweeds. We drove along the coast at first and then took a dirt road north that brought us through a cavernous area, to which, only after about thirty minutes, we stopped.

"See that bridge up there that crosses the cavern?" Ibn asked.

I looked toward the brightly lit area. "Yes, I see it."

"That is the border. If you cross here in the darkness, you could get over without being seen."

"But how could I? I don't have a flashlight or any idea which way to go!"

Ibn looked exasperated. "I promised only to take you to the border."

"But surely you wouldn't leave a woman out here alone! There could be wild animals in that cavern!"

Ibn put his head on the steering wheel and groaned something in his native language. "You are trouble," he said then.

He got out of the car then and opened the trunk. Out of it he took a large flashlight and a rifle. He motioned for me to get out of the car.

I hesitated. I wasn't sure if he was going to give them to me or shoot me.

"Come on," he said. "I will take you across."

I followed the man over the rocky terrain, thanking the Lord all the while that Ibn was at least a conscientious man and so far, I was unharmed.

"Allah, help us," Ibn said at one point, as we crossed an open space within view of the bridge.

At last we rounded a large pile of boulders and we were out of sight of the bridge. I let out a sigh of relief and Ibn turned and looked at me.

"Soon we will come to a little village on the shore," he said. "There you can find lodging for the night."

"Do they have a hotel?"

Ibn laughed. "No Missy. But they will take care of you."

"Why would they do that?"

"They are very devout people. The Qur'an teaches to be hospitable to strangers. You will see."

We came upon the village shortly and Ibn turned to me. "My five hundred dollars, please," he said.

I took out the money and handed it to him. "Thank you, Ibn," I said sincerely, "you've been a great help."

He looked at the ground sheepishly and then said, "I will help you find lodging."

He led me then down a row of little concrete block houses. He stopped at one that was neat and displayed a carefully weeded garden on its side.

"Here," he said with a smile. "Here you will stay."

He knocked at the door and after a moment it was opened by a little gray-haired woman, wearing a scarf over her head. Ibn greeted her in Arabic. After a few moments of discussion, the old woman stood aside and waved her arm for me to enter. Ibn bid us farewell and was gone.

I entered the little home, gratefully bowing while I removed the chador from my head. The woman looked surprised to see my blond hair and reached out to touch it.

After she closed the door, the old woman motioned for me to sit down on the floor before a crude but clean low table. She brought some bread with oil to dip, a sliced cucumber, and a glass of milk. Then she sat down beside me to watch me eat.

I wasn't sure about the food, but I wanted her to know that I appreciated her hospitality.

"Thank you," I said, wondering if she could understand.

She smiled and nodded her head toward the food.

I folded my hands and bowed my head to pray, "Thank you Lord for this food, for bringing me here safely, and for this kind woman. Amen."

"Amen," the woman said also.

I looked up at her in surprise. "Do you understand English?" I asked.

She just smiled and pointed at the food.

I didn't realize how hungry I was till I took the first bite. The panfried bread was fresh and almost warm and the oil was seasoned with herbs and garlic. It was delicious.

"It's very good," I told the woman, and she seemed to understand.

After the meal she brought me to a little room just off the main living quarters. On the floor there was a mat with blankets folded neatly on top of it. She waved her hand graciously toward them and again I gave her my thanks.

That night, as I lay on the little mat, I gazed toward the stars that shone through the window and marveled that I had come this far. What were General Pierce and Ivan thinking now? Did Walt know of my escapade?

I really wasn't trying to cause trouble. This was just something I had to do, and I would bring Walt the story of my career. Surely, they would see that my motives were good, though my actions may have been reckless. What harm could I do?

And hadn't the Lord delivered me safely? What were the odds of that were He not giving His providence and protection?

I thanked Him then and prayed for my husband. Perhaps tomorrow I would see my John! What joy that would bring me! It would be worth any sacrifice, just to say that I loved him and to display the depth of my feelings, by the risks that I took. With these noble thoughts, I closed my eyes and found sweet rest.

Eleven

The next morning at dawn, I awoke to the sound of the muezzin's call from the minaret of the mosque, singing in Arabic for his fellow Muslims to arise to prayer. It was a strange song to me, but beautiful in a way. The muezzin's voice was flawless and the gentle rhythm was soothing and made a peaceful entry into the day.

I knew that prayer in Islam was not a voluntary service in some parts of the world, and that this being a "devout" Islamic village, it would no doubt be an obligation or a law. Knowing this, I wanted to see the villagers' response to the call to prayer, so I stood up to look out of the window. Sure enough, the streets were littered with men beginning their day, lying prostrate toward Mecca; chanting from the Al Fatiha, their prayers of submission and for guidance.

I thought that Christians could take lessons in prayer from some of these Muslims. For though their prayer was offered in vain to a god that does not exist, their devotion could be seen visibly on the faces of some of these humble servants of Allah. It broke my heart to see this. Such worship they offer, with no guarantee from the Qur'an that their worship will be accepted or rewarded, or that they can even know for sure what their eternity holds.

The need for a missionary to come here and show them the way gripped my heart and tears began to fill my eyes. I went to my knees then and began to pray.

"Dear Lord," I began. "Can one soul give so much of his heart and life to a false god without Your notice? Surely you see these, on their knees and crying out so faithfully to—a god who cannot save and never promised that he would! A god that never showed his love or demonstrated the worth that each of these have within them—the worth that You see and valued above all that is in heaven! Oh Lord, send someone to show to them Your love and teach them the way of salvation."

My heart groaned within me as I said the words and when I had finished, I wiped the tears from my eyes and picked up my Bible. It fell open to Psalms, chapter two, and I read verse eight, which I had highlighted some time before, which read, "Ask of me, and I shall give thee the heathen for thine inheritance, and the uttermost parts of the earth for thy possession."

"Oh," I said, closing my Bible quickly, "surely you wouldn't want me. . . ." And as those words came from my mouth, I knew the hypocrisy of my prayer. I wanted these people to know and be able to worship the true and living God, but not enough to surrender my own life and dreams to see it happen.

This is too much for me to think about now, I thought then. I have to get to Basra.

I stood and began to busy myself with tidying the room and myself, all the while trying to ignore the still small voice that was gently tugging at my heart.

I left the room then with my things and saw the old woman, sitting on a little stool grinding meal. She stopped when she saw me and motioned again for me to sit before her humble table. Again, she brought some bread and oil, and this time, a bowl of sliced fruit to have with it. I wished very much to be able to communicate to her my thanks and did as best I could.

The need to get to Basra from here was my main concern after I had finished the simple breakfast. If only I could tell this woman, perhaps she could help me. I would pay her of course, and not presume upon her, but how to tell her this was beyond me.

A thought came to mind and I laid my laptop on the table and opened it up. It had a fully charged battery and I turned it on in order to retrieve my mother-in-law's address from within it.

The old woman's eyes were wide as I did this, and I could see that she was marveling at the contraption before me. I wrote the address on a slip of paper and handed it to her.

She looked at the paper in confusion.

"I need to go there," I said, pointing to myself and then to the paper.

She seemed to understand this and stood and left the room. A few minutes later she returned with a young man, to whom she spoke fervently to in Arabic.

I stood up then and reached into my bag to find my wallet. I did this and then presented the young man with fifty dollars in cash.

He looked at the money, at me, and then at the old woman. She pushed the money away while shaking her head.

"But I can pay . . . ," I said, feeling helpless to be understood.

The old woman smiled and patted my hand. She said something I didn't understand, except the word "Allah."

I looked at her in the eye and pointed to heaven. "May the Lord Jesus bless you and bring you His salvation," I said, emphasizing the name of the Lord.

She smiled again and then took my arm and led me to the front door. The young man and I stepped outside and I turned and extended my hand to shake hers. She took my hand and placed both of hers around it, and in her own tongue, bid me farewell.

Thankful for the kindness I had been shown, I turned from the old woman's home, placed my chador over my head, secured my black robe, and followed the young man to a little old car parked just around the corner. He opened the back door for me and I got inside.

As we drove along the arid countryside, I marveled at the fact that I was actually in Iraq! Who would have thought it possible and what reporter wouldn't envy my position now. I studied the landscape, taking mental notes for the story that I would write. Everything seemed so peaceful. One would never guess the hostile intentions that were brewing so near.

The young man who escorted me seemed very kind and quiet—not at all the stereotypical young male Arab that comes first to mind during a conflict such as this. He wore no turban around his head and his clothes were those of any Westerner. On his youthful face he wore glasses that made him appear studious, and I wondered if perhaps he was indeed a student.

"Excuse me," I asked, hoping to find out a little about him. "What is your name?"

He looked at me through the rear view mirror with a question on his face.

"I'm Sarah Morgan," I said, pointing to myself. "Sarah."

"Oh!" he responded with understanding. "Yes. I am Labib."

"Labib! That's wonderful!"

"Yes, yes."

"Labib, do you understand English?"

"No . . . only little," he answered with so heavy an accent that I hardly understood him.

"Do you go to school?"

"Yes. I am student . . . engineering."

"Where do you go to school?"

He looked at me without understanding, shrugging his shoulders.

"What town, city, place do you study?" I tried again slowly.

"Oh, Basra!"

"Oh, good! That's where we're going."

"Yes. I go to school," he answered and then turned to concentrate on driving.

Apparently, he had to go to Basra anyway this morning for classes. This made me feel more relaxed as my presence wasn't too great of an imposition.

"What time is your class?" I asked pointing to my watch.

He looked at me again puzzled, trying to understand my question.

"Oh," he said then, as it dawned on him, "Two hours."

I nodded my head and sat back in my seat. Two hours would be plenty of time to drop me off and then be on his way to his own business, I thought happily. And I would indeed pay him for his time.

Shortly thereafter, we began to see the outlying area of the city of Basra. It was not at all what I expected. The city was modern and beautiful, with lush greenery growing in abundance along a river that it sat beside, which was so large, it seemed more like the sea.

"This is a beautiful city!" I said to Labib.

Labib shook his head. I wasn't sure if he understood or not.

As we drove into the city, I peered out of the window in wonder at this old but new to me culture, that reminded me so of some exotic movie or book that I had read. Every other man looked like one of the "forty thieves" in their long robes and turbans, and I wondered if concealed underneath their flowing garments there were kept sharp sabers or perhaps a knife. These thoughts made the place seem all the more ominous and a little exciting as well.

Labib seemed to know just where he was going and before long he pulled up before a large, government–looking building.

"We are here," he said to me, while holding up the address that I had provided.

"What is this?" I asked.

"It is post office," answered Labib.

"Post office! But this is no good!"

"It is address you gave."

"Oh . . . " I said slowly, thinking what to do. "Will you come inside with me?"

"Yes."

We went inside and I got in line to speak with a clerk. Labib followed me, and when we reached the counter, I asked him to ask the clerk if he knew of the lady who rented the box.

Labib looked at me skeptically. "So many people in city," he said shaking his head. "It is not very hopeful."

"Please ask anyway," I begged.

Labib spoke to the man in Arabic for a little while, then another man joined them and began to speak in hushed tones. Labib turned from them with a worried look on his face and then motioned for me to follow him to a private corner.

"Did they know who she was?" I asked with anticipation when we were alone.

"Sarah," he began, pronouncing my name in a way I'd never heard before. "You do not want to go to friend's abode."

"Of course I do," I answered. "It is my mother-in-law that I want to see."

"But it is not safe," he answered mysteriously.

"Does she live in a bad neighborhood, or what?" I asked.

He didn't seem to understand what I meant.

"Look, wherever it is, I'm not afraid to go there. I've been in rough situations before. It goes along with my job. And I'll pay you a hundred dollars to take me there."

"Oh, no!" Labib said shaking his head vigorously and folding his arms. "I'm not going near that place!"

"But you're my only friend here and I'm a lone woman," I entreated, placing a hand on his arm. "I would never find my way on my own."

Labib studied the ground for a moment with a furrowed brow. "Okay," he said finally. "I will take you close enough to get there by foot, but no further."

"Oh, thank you!" I said gratefully, repressing the desire to hug his neck.

Labib got in the car with the look of a man who had been convinced against his will. I hated playing the helpless female to win my objective, but it had been my only trump. Feeling guilty, I took out a hundred dollar bill and laid it on the seat. Somehow I knew he was a chivalrous young man and would not take it from my hand.

We drove away from the city a few miles and into the desert. I wondered at this and then thought perhaps my mother-in-law lived in an outlying suburb.

The sun was climbing higher in the sky by this time and though it was still mid-morning, the heat and humidity had started to become stifling. I took off the black robe and chador.

Suddenly we stopped in the middle of the desert.

"This is as far as I go," Labib said, and then got out of the car. He opened my door and I got out as well.

"But we're out in the middle of nowhere!" I exclaimed, while looking around.

Labib pointed far to the east. "There," he said. "There is where you want to go."

I looked toward the direction that he was pointing and there on the horizon I could just barely make out a trail of smoke.

"Couldn't you bring me a little closer?" I asked.

"No!" Labib answered firmly.

I could see that his mind was made.

He reached in the car then and handed me my things and my robe and head covering. "You better put that on," he said.

"Thank you, Labib," I said with resignation. "I will never forget your kindness."

He turned then, got in his car, and drove away.

And, so, there I stood in the middle of the desert with nothing but my computer and a few meager belongings. The improbability of it hit me suddenly and I had to laugh at myself. You had your way, Sarah, I thought to myself. Now let's see what you've gotten yourself into! And with that, I began to follow the trail of smoke.

Twelve

I had walked for about fifteen minutes, when I heard the sound of heavy steps coming up from behind me. I turned and saw that it was a camel, with a rider on top. The rider, an Arab man dressed in fatigues and a beige turban, saw me at the same time, and with a look of surprise on his face, he rode toward me and then forced the camel down so that he could get off.

He came so close to where I stood that I had to back up to see him clearly. As I backed up, he took a step closer and then again and again, until I realized that if I didn't stand still we'd be at this all day.

He stood then before me with his face close to mine and I turned my head to avoid his onion breath and offensive body odor. Then he jerked the chador from my head and made a sound of delight, while saying something in Arabic.

"Please," I said, backing away from him, "I'm going to see my mother-in-law. She lives over that way," I said, pointing toward the trail of smoke and hoping he could understand English.

Apparently, he did not and without warning, he grabbed me by the waist and swung me up on his camel. He got on behind me and I thought I would die as I felt his sweaty body touch mine. I struggled to get down for a moment, but with his strong arm about me and the camel's swift rise, I realized I was at his mercy.

With a hearty laugh, he smacked the camel with a rod, and we were off.

I don't think I'd ever been so afraid in all my life. My heart beat wildly and thoughts of harems and cruel masters filled my mind. I prayed a silent prayer for help, with the dawning realization that if I were in real trouble, no one in the world that cared for me knew where I was; and for that matter, I wasn't even exactly sure myself.

The one good thing was that he was heading toward the same location that I had been. Hopefully, the clerk at the post office had been correct and this was indeed where my mother-in-law resided. My future depended on it now!

It wasn't long before we were approaching our destination, and I gasped as it came into view. Surely, the man at the post office had made a mistake. My mother-in-law would never be able to live in these surroundings. This was obviously the home of a desert nomadic tribe! My mother-in-law had been a refined lady, with a home in the States to rival a diplomat. Here were only tents! Tents to be sure, that were durable and strong enough to endure fierce desert winds, but tents nonetheless. They were made of black goats' hair, shrunken and sewn tightly together, and reminded me of a verse in the Song of Solomon as it referred to the "tents of Kedar." I had read of the like such as this, but never in my wildest dreams did I think I would ever be in a place like this myself.

The clan was large and they pitched their tents in a giant circle, in which some of their flocks they kept protected within this enclosure of the camp. Along with the animals within that circle, the children played, while the women cooked over fire pits or pounded grain in hand mills. Hanging from poles were skin bags or bottles containing water or maybe other liquids.

As we arrived at the camp, my captor eased the camel down and roughly grabbed my arm, pulling me off the camels back. I clung tightly to my few belongings as he brought me into the circle of tents.

It was like stepping back in time to enter a community

such as this, and I felt conspicuous and out of place. All activity seemed to stop at my arrival, as women stood to their feet and children came to stare at my blond hair.

A child then ran into a tent, calling as he did and arousing the attention of a man who was inside. The man stepped out of his tent and his commanding presence dominated the surreal situation. He was an older man, dressed in a long white robe and turban that were decorated with gold chains and jewels. He was the sheik, no doubt, of this compound and would have the last word, I was certain, concerning me.

His attention was on me then and I could see by the look in his eye that he was immediately fascinated by my fair hair and complexion. He instructed the man who escorted me here to bring me to him. I was loath to stand before him and could not help but dig my heels into the sand. It was useless, of course, and soon I stood trembling beneath the speculative eye of this giant of a desert king.

The two men began to speak to one another in Arabic and I wished desperately to communicate to them the reason for my presence. When I gained their attention, I gave my mother-in-law's name and to my despair, they looked at one another and shrugged their shoulders.

With a laugh then the sheik grabbed my arm and dragged me into his tent. The other man gave some opposition, but was quickly dismissed by the condescending glare of the older man. I was brought through a main living quarter, which was quite grand, and then taken into another apartment which obviously served as a residence for the women and children who were the property of the sheik.

He tossed me toward a gray-haired woman, while giving her instructions concerning me, and then left. I was bewildered and afraid and wondered what this day would hold for me. The outlook was grim and when the woman began to pull me toward a large tub of water and reach to remove my clothes, I knew that I was in real trouble.

I struggled to free myself from her bony grip and as I did, several younger women came to her aid. They removed my clothes while I fought and then shoved me into the tub of lukewarm, gray water. With ahhs and sounds of wonder, they washed my blond hair and peered into my angry blue eyes. When the washing was over, they brought a large towel, for which I was thankful, and wrapped it around me. They sat me down then and shook and dried my hair and then proceeded to coil and braid it in some sort of arrangement that they thought suitable. I sat numb by this time and let them have their way.

When they finished with my hair, some "clothes" were brought for me to wear and it was then that my worst fears were confirmed. I was being prepared for the sheik. The "clothes" were nothing more than sheer fabric, sewn with seduction in mind. There would be no way in the world that anyone was going to force me to wear such as this in front of a man that was not my husband! As the women brought the garments toward me, I grabbed them from their hands and ripped with all my strength. They shrieked at my audacity of tearing their precious wrappings and soon began to pull them from my ravenous hands. Before I knew how it happened, there was kicking and scratching and I was involved in a vicious cat fight!

The screaming and yelling was deafening, until the sheik returned in a fury and ordered the escapade to cease. I tightened the towel around me indignantly and turned to face the rear of the tent. Some orders were given and the sheik left. Amazingly, my own clothes were returned to me and I was brought to a corner of the dwelling and given a mat on which to lie. I was extremely thankful for this reprieve and wondered how long it would be mine.

The other women stayed clear of me except to send angry glares as they nursed their scratches. After I had dressed, I lay down on the mat and began to quietly cry. What had I gotten myself into! Must I always rush into situations without forethought or planning? Was there a bigger fool in all the world than me? I had come to this place on only the word of a stranger, whose language I couldn't understand! My mother-in-law was probably a world away from this desert clan. With these thoughts, I cried for some time. I'm not sure at what point I fell asleep, but somehow I managed to.

Thirteen

I was awakened late in the afternoon by a beautiful melody drifting though the air. For a moment, I didn't know where I was. The piece was played expertly on a piano and seemed to me to be completely foreign to this part of the world. It was Beethoven's "Fur Elise."

Suddenly, I realized that this was my mother-in-law's favorite composition and I had heard her play it several times before. Could she be here somewhere playing this romantic concerto?

With that question, I began to call her name. The other women, who had been resting as well, awoke and began to try and quiet me. With every "Shh," I called louder until, as they started to rise and come toward me, I was yelling her name.

A commotion was then heard in the front apartment and soon, to my overwhelming relief, the curtains were parted and there stood my mother-in-law in all the dignity that I remembered her to possess. The respect she commanded was evident, which was an anomaly for certain in this part of the world, for she spoke only a word and I was handed over to her charge.

I reached to throw my arms around her then, and with graceful gesture, she turned me instead and led me out of the women's quarters. I followed like a quieted child and stifled the cries that choked in my throat. When we were finally outside I began to speak, but was held off by her warning look.

She walked through the camp with her head held high

and received from the other women, who sat working with the grain or preparing food, a revered nod or look of astonished admiration. She did not smile back at them or turn her head from her determined course. She was like a queen whose own self respect was assumed by all those she came in contact with.

She wore a scarf over her head and a long flowing robe, but it was not the black chador that adorned every other woman including myself. It was a silken wrap of deep purples and etched with silver that framed her still lovely face, and gave her the look of royalty. How she managed this variance was a mystery, and I wondered at what cost she had obtained such privilege.

At last, we entered her tent and I gave in to the tears that sat in restraint. My mother-in-law held me then while I cried, and smoothed my hair as she whispered words of comfort.

When I had dried my tears, she brought me to a lounging area that consisted of a group of large colorful pillows, that sat on a mat in a semicircle and were draped overhead by sheer curtains. We sat down in this comfortable enclosure and she took me then by the hands and looked into my face.

"Dear child," she said softly in perfect English, "how in the world did you get here and why?"

I reached in my bag and pulled out my press badge. "I'm here on assignment. The hostage crisis, you know."

Her eyes were wide as she said, "How could your newspaper put you in such a dangerous position!"

I looked down at my badge. "Well, actually . . . I took it upon myself to come this far. They sent me only as far as the military base in the Persian Gulf."

"Oh, Sarah!" she said emphatically then. "Do you not realize the precarious position you are in? Are you so ambitious in your work as to risk your precious life for the sake of an exclusive story?!"

Sarah's Folly

"Oh, Mother!" I said then with tears threatening to surface once more. "I didn't come here for an exclusive story! I came here for John! I think he may be one of the hostages!"

I went on then to recount to her the whole story. The fight we had, the weeks of searching, the entire set of circumstances that brought me to this place.

When I had finished, she stood and turned from me and began an obvious thoughtful struggle.

"What is it?" I said. "Do you know something about John?"

She turned and looked at me. "Sarah," she said with feeling, "I never knew the depth of love you held for my son. I can't tell you how much that means to me."

There was something more that she wasn't telling me. I could sense it, but I could not probe, for I was taken back at her show of emotion. I had never seen her cry before. She was like a stoic matriarch who had mastered her responses to the point of perfect control. It was so out of character for her to be overcome, that I was amazed.

She came and sat beside me again. "Sarah," she said while taking my hand, "I loved John's father that way. I would have done anything for him. It was my dearest wish for my son to have the treasure of true love as well. I had hoped that he had found it in you, but I didn't know for sure. I do now." She reached over and kissed me on my forehead and then said, "Thank you."

"I do love him so much!" I cried. "And I must find him to let him know, before it's too late!"

"I understand," she answered, looking off as into a faraway place. "I met John's father, and fell in love in similar circumstances—in a time of turmoil."

"I didn't know."

"Yes, it was in the early seventies, after Iraq was fully nationalized and enjoying great prosperity through the discovery of major oil deposits in the region. With this money

92

they made large contributions to aid Syria during the Arab-Israeli war of October 1973. They not only aided them with material, but also with men. Some of my family were sent to fight. One of them was hurt, my brother, and I went to the border to see how bad he was."

"Your parents allowed it?!" I asked.

"They didn't know," she answered in kindred spirit.

I looked at her in wonder.

"You see, I do understand how love can make one careless. When you're young, you think life will go on forever. It's not until you begin to lose friends and loved ones that you realize what a precious gift life is and how little time we really have to make a difference in this world."

"So, you met your husband when you went to the border?"

"Yes. He was a Marine, like John, and was sent by his country to aid Israel," she said and smiled at the memory. "I had wandered, unknowing, into enemy territory. He saw me and came to try and help me get back where I belonged. I spoke a little English and resisted his help at first, but then came to realize that I was in real danger. He protected me and tried for weeks to get me home. And then one day I didn't want to go home. I saw that this man I was with was the finest man I'd ever known. He never took advantage of me when he could have and saw that no one else did either. He had a respect for me that was foreign to women in this part of the world. I had never been treated with such kindness and deference. But more than that, it was his faith in his God that arrested my attention. He had more than just a fidelity to a merciless god who demanded ritual praying, as I had witnessed growing up. He had a relationship with his Lord, as a son would with a father and a love for Him that was genuine."

"Did he share his faith with you then?" I asked.

"Yes, every night around the campfire he would take his Bible and tell me the story of Jesus. And one night I bowed my head and received His God as my own. It was the most wonderful night of my life."

"And then you fell in love."

"Yes," she answered softly. "And then we fell in love."

"What happened after that?"

"Well, when the time came for his leave, he took me to Cairo and we were married. When he went back to the States, I went with him."

"How did your family respond to that?" I asked in wonder.

"They were appalled, of course. They hated Americans. But as the years went by and my husband was good to me and them, they began to soften."

"But these people seem so savage! You should have seen what that sheik had in mind for me! I still don't understand how you managed to get me out of there."

"Well you see, the sheik is my brother. The one I went to the border for."

I stared at her in amazement.

"We were very close as children," she said with a note of tenderness in her voice. "And when my father died and he became the sheik, he was faced then with certain financial disaster. The flocks were sick and dying and he had no resources to make them well or replenish the dwindling herds. My husband sent, at that time, a substantial gift to get him on his feet and with that forever won his acceptance."

"So he doesn't hate Americans any longer?" I assumed.

"Oh no," she said emphatically. "He hates them now more than ever. It was just my husband he accepted, deeming him different from the rest."

"Oh," I answered slowly. "What did you say then to him about me?"

"I told him you were my husband's relation, here to see me."

"I'm surprised he let me go with just that."

"He was suspicious."

"I thought for a moment I was going to forever be part of some harem!"

"You have to understand that it is their way of life. They are not Christians and it is permitted in the Qur'an."

"How could you come back here and live in such an environment as this?"

"Well, you see," she answered with a creased brow, "when I ran off to be married, I always felt as if I had abandoned my family. But more than anything else, I wanted to be able to show them the way of salvation through our Lord Jesus. When my husband died, and my mother fell sick, I felt it was right for me to return and take care of her and try to win her and my family to Christ."

"Have you succeeded?"

"No," she answered sadly. "They are very much against it and my brother has forbidden me to speak of my faith to the clan."

I looked at my mother-in-law with new understanding and respect. She had forfeited a great deal to bring the gospel to her people and her willingness to set aside personal comforts to aid her mother in her time of need was praiseworthy. I wondered how I would respond in similar circumstances.

"I will do my best to be a good testimony while I'm here," I told her.

"That will be essential," she said.

After a pause, I looked at her seriously and asked, "And what do you think I should do about John?"

"I don't think that there is very much you can do," she answered.

"But I need to reach him. If only just to speak to him for a moment."

"My dear," she said kindly, "don't you realize that he knows how you feel about him? He knows, in the same way that you know, without being told, that he loves you."

"But I said that I didn't love him the last time we were together!"

"In the heat of an argument, as you said. I am certain that he understands that your true self was not in evidence that day. Your emotions were distorted by anger and could not be taken as sincere."

"Then why did he leave the way he did?" I cried. "With no word or even a note of where he had gone!"

She gathered me in her arms and patted my hair. "He must have had a very good reason."

I pulled away from her and stood to my feet. "But I need to know," I said desperately. "I thought you could help me!"

She stood as well and looked me firmly in the eye. "I'm sorry, Sarah," she said. "There's nothing I can do."

Fourteen

The next morning I awoke in the dark sprawling tent of my mother-in-law. After a while, a flood of light filled the room and I saw that she had lifted the front opening for the day. For a tent, it was actually quite a pleasant dwelling. The main room was decorated from top to bottom with beautiful sheer curtains, colorful pillows, and oriental pottery of various shapes and sizes. Persian rugs dominated the floors and there, sitting conspicuously to one side, was my mother-in-law's shiny grand piano. I wondered how she had gotten it here.

"Wake up, Sarah!" she called then. "Come and have breakfast with my mother and me."

I wrapped the robe around me that she had provided, moved the curtain aside that enclosed my sleeping area, and walked over to where they sat at the low table. The food smelled delicious.

"Bacon and eggs!" I said with surprise.

"You like eggs, don't you?" my mother-in-law asked.

"Yes, of course. I just didn't expect it."

I sat down then at the table and my mother-in-law proceeded to introduce me to her mother.

"Sarah, I want you to meet my mom," she said and then turned to the older woman clad in black and began to speak to her in her own tongue.

I smiled at the grandmother who had lost the privilege of watching my husband grow up and was suddenly sad at the thought. But of course, he would be a different person today had he been raised here and I might never have known him. It seemed her loss was my gain and I felt in her debt.

The grandmother looked at me through squinted eyes after the introduction, and without an acknowledgment or greeting, turned to her food and began to eat. It appeared that I was not welcome where she was concerned.

"What did you tell her?" I asked my mother-in-law.

"The same thing I told the others, that you are my husband's relation."

"Why didn't you tell her that I was your son's wife?"

"I thought it would be best not to."

"Why?" I asked with a puzzled expression.

She patted my hand and whispered, "You'll have to trust me, Sarah. I need to protect you."

I still didn't get it. It was my nationality, of course, but prejudice was so foreign to my thinking that I had a hard time understanding it. I was brought up to see it as absurd and believed firmly in the maxim that all men were created equal.

The grandmother then, while nodding in my direction, made some kind of angry statement to my mother-in-law. She responded in gentleness and then turned to smile at me.

"It will be all right," she said.

I wondered if it would.

She looked at my solemn expression and said with encouragement, "After breakfast, I have a surprise for you."

"Oh?"

"It should cheer you up."

Later, my mother-in-law took me by the hand and brought me outside and around to the back of the encampment. There, to my surprise was a late-model car!

"Is this yours?" I asked with wide eyes.

"Yes!" she answered. "You didn't think I'd get around on a camel did you?"

"I really didn't have any idea."

"Although, I probably still could manage one if the need arose!" she said with a chuckle.

"I don't think anything you did would surprise me now!" I said smiling.

"I'll take that as a compliment."

"I meant it as one."

"Get in," she said then.

"Where are we going?" I asked, as I opened the car door and slid inside.

"To Basra."

"Will they let you?"

"Only my brother would try to stop me. He thinks I'm going shopping."

"Will he mind?"

"Not if I bring him back some Turkish Delights," she said with a smile.

The bustling city of Basra was not very far and soon we were coming upon the lush green foliage that bordered the great body of water that she sat against.

"We'll have lunch later in a nice restaurant that overlooks the water," my mother-in-law said. "They have great food and a wonderful view."

"Where are we going now?"

"I actually do need to do a little shopping, but the main reason for our trip into town is to attend a meeting that my church is conducting later today. I thought you might enjoy it."

"Your church?"

"Yes. It's an underground Baptist mission work, in fact."

"What kind of meeting is it?"

"A revival meeting of sorts."

"Do they really have to meet in secret?"

"Yes, the government doesn't look kindly on a work such as ours."

"Is there any danger where the missionaries are concerned?"

"There could be. So far, however, we've not had any trouble."

"Does your brother know about your involvement with the mission?"

"No," she answered with force. "He'd kill me if he did!"

"Do you really think he'd kill you?"

"Well, I don't know if he would actually kill me, but he would be mad enough to."

"Do you spend much time there?"

"As much as I can. It keeps me going and focused on what I'm doing here. It's the highlight of my week to meet with my brothers and sisters in Christ."

I smiled at her with understanding. It will be good for me as well to sit under the preaching of the Word.

"Thank you for bringing me," I told her. "This will be the first foreign mission work that I will have the privilege to see. I'm looking forward to it."

After we spent some time shopping, which was an extraordinary experience in itself, we made our way to the well-known restaurant that sat on the waterway. It had quite a pleasant dining area, with its Persian motif and spectacular view.

As we sat looking at our menus, I said to my mother-in-law, "You'll have to order for me. This menu's in Arabic!"

"Oh, yes, of course," she smiled and said. "I'll take care of you."

She ordered the food and then turned to me and said kindly, "You know, Sarah, this is the first time I've had the opportunity to spend time with you alone. I'm pleased to get to know you better, in spite of the extenuating circumstances."

"Me, too," I said shyly. "I have admired you from the first time I saw you, but never did I realize the depth of your love for the Lord. I mean . . . I knew you were saved, but I thought the spiritual influence in John's life stemmed mainly from his father."

"He was definitely the spiritual leader in our home," she said humbly. "But now that I'm alone, I've come to lean heavily on the Lord myself and I've found Him to be all sufficient for my every heart's need. I love Him truly and beyond even the love I had for my dear husband and son."

The gravity and sincerity of her words astounded me and I sat in silence wondering if I could ever feel the same.

"It is for that reason that I am so thankful for my church." she said. "There's nothing that swells my heart more than to sing praises to my Lord and to hear His name lifted high and exalted."

"Tell me more about the pastor," I asked then.

"Well," she answered thoughtfully, "he is a young man, born in Iraq and led to the Lord by an Arab pastor who ministers to Arab-Christians in Jerusalem. He and his wife attended Bible college in the States and have been here for five years working to establish this work in Basra."

"Do they have children?"

"No," she smiled answering, "I think they are a little afraid to."

"Because of the work they do?"

"Yes, although they have never told me so."

"But you said there hasn't been any trouble with the mission."

"No, not yet," she answered soberly. "But you see, all mission outreach in Muslim lands is condemned. To convert a Muslim to another faith is considered a crime more serious than murder."

"Oh, no," I said with concern.

"Yes, you see mission work among Muslims is considered an assault on the Muslim government and an attempt to undermine or overthrow its authority."

"I've read that the ultimate aim of Islam is a religious state, but I still don't understand what faith has to do with politics?"

"In the Muslim mind, it has everything to do with it," she answered emphatically. "You see, the original purpose of Islam was not so much to bridge the gap between god and man, but rather to bridge the gap between men with men."

"Explain what you mean."

"You see, in the days of the Muslim prophet Muhammad, there were serious social concerns that were apparent in that day. The poor were starving and the rich were increasing in goods by taking advantage of them. The Qur'an was given to Muhammad, as he claimed, to bring justice to the poor and equity in practical matters such as family life, inheritances, business contracts, legalities, war, slavery, penalties, along with the spiritual demands of Allah."

"So, it was more of a means of social reform," I concluded.

"It was a means of bringing order and purpose to Arab peoples," she said. "Something that they were in desperate need of."

"Why is that?"

"You see, the Arabs were at that time, and still are to some extent, a people whose tribe or clan was all important; and the feuds between them prevented their communities from prospering the way other peoples did who could participate with one another. They were backward and primitive compared to the rest of the world. Not only that, they were spiritually starving in spite of the pagan worship that dominated the land."

"Why didn't they look to the Bible for life's answers?"

"They did, in fact, long for a faith as trustworthy, strong, and historically consistent as the Jews' and Christians', but with such hostilities that they felt toward those of their own race, you can only imagine the prejudices they had for those outside of their own nationality. To assume the Jews' or Christians' way of life, or to accept the Savior, was an impossible affront to their ancestral pride."

"So, they needed a religion of their own," I concluded.

"Yes, with rules to live by and a prophet to lead them."

"So, Muhammad filled a gaping void for his people in his day."

"Yes, and set in motion a force that would change the course of history and turn the hearts of men from the redemption that God provided through our Lord Jesus Christ."

"Doesn't the Qur'an mention Jesus?"

"Yes, but only as a prophet. A man that Muhammad put on the same, or lower level than himself, and failed to declare as the Lamb of God, who takes away the sin of the world."

"How could any man put God's Son on the same level as themselves?"

"It has been done again and again throughout history. The Bible warns that false prophets would arise and that we should reject them."

"Do you think that Muhammad really believed that he was a prophet?"

"It's hard to say what went on in his mind from the time he first began to have 'visitations.'"

"I've read that these 'visitations' were described as a type of 'seizure' that many scholars suggest were the result of epilepsy," I said.

"Yes, I've read that too," my mother-in-law agreed, "and tradition records that Muhammad would fall to the ground, roll and jerk around, while he would foam at the mouth and his eyes would roll backwards when he was about to receive a revelation."

"It sounds almost like he was demon possessed."

My mother-in-law grimaced. "That has also been suggested, although I like to think otherwise. In fact, history records that Muhammad's mother, Aminah, often claimed that she had been visited by spirits or *jinns* and was involved in what we would call today the 'occult arts.' Muhammad said that he received visitations even as a child and it makes one wonder how much of an influence his mother's practices had on him, because she died when he was only six."

"Why are you opposed to this notion, Mother?" I asked.

"Probably because I was brought up to revere and respect the Muslim prophet so much that it just goes against my training," she said honestly. "I know that doesn't make sense."

I gave an understanding nod.

"I like to think," she continued, "that Muhammad's visions were the result of an overworked imagination and the excuse to cover his embarrassment over his physical condition. That, combined with an honest effort to help his people find a better way of life, is a more reasonable explanation to me."

"What do you make of the distorted Bible stories that are recorded in the Qur'an?" I asked.

"It is possible that they were intentionally rewritten and misrepresented by Muhammad in order to fit his particular religious ideas. But there is also the possibility that he never heard them told correctly. You see, Muhammad was illiterate, and because he could not read, he had to rely on hearsay and the stories of others in order to learn. He had contact with Jews and Christians at various times through his job as a tradesman, and also with some who lived nearby. The city of Mecca, where he lived, also housed the Kabah, which was a center of worship for the entire region and boasted three hundred sixty different idols, along with the sacred black stone, which was considered to be sort of a 'good luck charm' for his tribe, the Quraysh. When he began to write—or rather recite—his religious work, the Qur'an, I concur that he created a mixture of the things he liked best about the religious jargon he heard around him from his youth, and formed a religion and a god all his own."

"What do you think the sacred black stone is?" I asked.

"It is said to be a meteorite," my mother-in-law answered. "Muhammad revered the stone so much because he grew up near the Kabah and would watch the cultic practice performed every year as the 'pilgrims' would come to worship by running around it seven times, kissing the black stone, and then running down to nearby Wadi to throw stones at the devil. When he and his religion gained the power to do so, he destroyed all of the idols, save this one, and made this pagan worship a part of the five pillars of his faith."

"It is called the *'Hajj,'* isn't it."

"Yes, or the pilgrimage to Mecca. Every Muslim must attempt to make this journey once in a lifetime and do the same pagan worship that Muhammad had witnessed as a child."

"It seems so ludicrous," I commented.

"Yes, it does."

"It's a shame that Muhammad could not have found the Lord through the Christians he came in contact with."

"I agree," my mother-in-law said thoughtfully. "Although, I wonder if he ever did receive a clear witness. He obviously did not understand who God was or the Lord Jesus. It's obvious also, however, that somehow God's Word rang true to him. He referred in the Qur'an to the Torah and the Gospel as 'guidance to the people.' Another time he said, 'People of the Book, you do not stand on anything, until you perform the Torah and the Gospel.' Yet even with this respect for the Bible, he failed to recognize its most crucial point in the plan and objective of God, that is, to provide redemption for mankind through the Messiah. The prophecies that the Lord Jesus fulfilled are indisputable and impossible to ignore if one will just consider them. But Muhammad could not read Arabic, much less Hebrew or Greek, and had he been able to, he may have been like the Ethiopian whom Philip was sent to and whom Philip asked when he saw him reading the prophecies in Isaiah concerning Christ: 'Understandest thou what thou readest?' and the Ethiopian answered, 'How can I, except some man should guide me?' That man was saved because of Philip's clear witness and his obedience to give that witness. I often wonder how different the world would be if this man Muhammad would have received a witness so clear, and received it. But equally important now, is that my people hear. That is the objective of my life."

At this juncture, the waiter came and brought our food. We gave thanks to the Lord for it and began to eat.

"This is very good," I said as I ate the combination of fish, onions, and herbs over rice.

"Mine is also," my mother-in-law said. "They have a very fine chef here."

While we ate, I asked my mother-in-law what she thought about the *Satanic Verses* that were so highly publicized because of Salman Rushdie's controversial book.

"The *Satanic Verses* are not the invention of that author," she replied. "They originated from Muhammad himself. You see, Muhammad was not well received in his hometown. The city of Mecca, as I mentioned before, was a place of worship for most of the Arabian peninsula for a long time. Many of his own tribe benefited from the idolatrous shrines and altars as they gained wealth from the pilgrims who came there to worship. When Muhammad began to publicly criticize and mock the pilgrims and their idols and say that there was no god but his, his own tribe began to persecute him and even kill some of his followers. When the persecutions became intense at one point, he gave in to the Meccan leaders by having a convenient revelation that declared that perhaps Allah could have had a wife, Al-lat, and two daughters, Al-Uzza and Manat, who were considered to be gods as well at that time. The town leaders were satisfied with that and things returned to normal. His followers, however, were disappointed and Muhammad came to regret the compromise. He said that he had listened to the whisperings of Satan and that he considered his words in Sura, The Star, to be 'satanic verses.' Salman Rushdie alluded to this story in an obscure work of fiction that the Muslims took great offense to and they made it the duty of any Muslim who encountered Rushdie to kill him for his 'blasphemous' book."

"That's interesting," I said. "And how did the Meccans respond to Muhammad's confession that his previous revelation was of Satan."

"Persecution returned and Muhammad had to eventually flee for his life."

"How ever did that religion survive?" I asked.

"They had a hard time, of course. Muhammad had to seek refuge among other than his own peoples at different times. He was once protected by the Christian community of Abyssinia, and made yet another compromise as he convinced them that his religion was not unlike their own. They offered compassion and sustenance, but in their ignorance, failed to evangelize Muhammad and his followers.

"That reminds me of mission works that only concern themselves with social care and not a Christian testimony or teaching," I said sadly.

"Yes, and in the end, the Christians in Abyssinia actually rescued Islam!" my mother-in-law said with amazement.

"They could never have known the impact that that man of destiny, whom they nurtured in their bosoms, would make against Christianity," I said. "Probably not even Muhammad himself knew."

"Surely not," my mother-in-law said. "The Muslims were still just hanging on for their lives until Muhammad received an invitation to come to Medina as a ruler. It was there that Muhammad received his first opportunity to prove himself as a statesman."

"Why would the people of Medina invite someone who was not of their own tribe to come and rule over them?" I asked.

"Well, you see, the city of Medina was comprised of several different clans who were attempting to work together to create a prosperous community. They needed a common denominator to bring the disjointed tribes together and create some sort of harmony. They had heard of Muhammad and his new system of combined government and religion and it appealed to them. They all agreed to become Muslim if Muhammad would come and rule over them."

"Muhammad must have been ecstatic with an invitation like that!" I mused.

"I'm sure he was," my mother-in-law agreed. "It turned out to be the turning point for Islam. Before, Muhammad had been viewed as a contemptible prophet, but in Medina he was given the status of a superior ruler. It was here that the Muslims regard the establishment of the new religion, where their beliefs took shape in a political form."

"So, all went well for Muhammad after that?"

"Not exactly. After the excitement died down of arriving in Medina with such open arms, Muhammad was faced with serious problems for the followers who had come with him to Medina. Their goods and funds had been confiscated by the Meccans and they had to rely on the hospitality of the Medinans in order to survive. You can imagine how long that could go on."

I nodded my head in response.

"It was then that the infamous 'holy war' took shape in the mind of Muhammad and he began to try and incite his people, in the name of Allah, to attack and plunder the traveling caravans of Mecca to relieve their financial stress."

"How did his followers feel about that?"

"They were against it. The people that they would be attacking were their own kinsmen and blood bonds among Arabs were highly valued."

"How did he ever talk them into it?"

"He had a difficult time. He succeeded in forming a

fighting band, but when it came to the time of attack, they all abandoned Muhammad."

"What did he do then?"

"At first, he tried to rally his men with direct commands from Allah. Then he tried enticing them with the booty that they would receive. He cursed them, insulted them, threatened and did just about everything to motivate his followers to attack. But they refused."

"Good for them!"

"Eventually, Muhammad focused his attention on some of his wilder companions and was able to persuade them to attack. At first, they were unsuccessful and so Muhammad decided to wait before they attacked again till a time when they could catch their prey by surprise. So he waited until the month of pilgrimage, when all fighting among the Arabs was forbidden under treaty, and then he drove his men to treacherously attack an unarmed caravan."

"How did his peace-loving followers react to that?"

"They were angry and condemned the attack. They even refused to accept the pillage. But Muhammad understood them and he had a plan to weaken their resolve."

"What did he do?"

"He commanded that the camels should remain loaded with the booty and left in the town square. After observing the rich supply of goods for several days, the people changed their minds."

"Smart move," I chuckled, "working on their greed."

"He also convinced them, by having another 'revelation' that this was the will of Allah."

"So this is how the notorious 'holy wars' began."

"Yes," she agreed. "After that success, raiding and plundering became their way of sustaining themselves. Through it, they became rich and then when riches were no longer necessary, they began to conquer villages and force the people to become Muslim. As Muhammad's group grew wealthy, others would join them in order to take part in the profits. Soon, Muhammad had conquered most all of his world, including his hometown of Mecca."

"Wow, that's some story," I commented.

"Yes, and it continues to go on to this day, as Muslim terrorists still firmly believe that Allah has commanded them to bring nations to him by means of force. In some Islamic countries, people are forced to pray to Allah at gunpoint when the muezzins call."

"And the young Muslim men of this century will still risk their lives for these 'holy wars'?"

"Absolutely," my mother-in-law affirmed. "Muhammad taught his people that the only sure way to enter paradise after death, was to die in a 'holy war.' "

"What a legacy of terror Muhammad left to his people!"

"Yes, and the rest of the world, for that matter," my mother-in-law said.

I looked thoughtfully out of the window for a moment.

"Muhammad seemed to have many 'revelations' of convenience," I commented. "How could all of his followers buy his claim that they were dictated from Allah?"

"He did, in fact have many 'revelations of convenience' as you call them," my mother-in-law answered wryly. "Some, much more hard to believe than the ones we have spoken of."

"Such as?"

"Well, once he even had the nerve to demand that the much-loved wife of his adopted son, Zaid, whom he desired because of her great beauty, be given to him and backed his demand by a 'revelation' that he actually included in a Sura!"

"Did his son give him his wife?"

"At first he refused and said the request was outrageous, which was true. But eventually Zaid and his wife were forced to comply. They had to submit to the will of Allah."

110   "That's amazing!"

"Yes, it is," my mother-in-law agreed. "But there was at least one man who tried and succeeded to get Muhammad to make changes in some parts of Muhammad's 'revelations.'"

"Oh?"

"His name was Abdollah Sarh, and he would often suggest to Muhammad that he add, subtract, or rephrase portions of his Suras."

"And Muhammad took his advice?"

"Yes, but as it turned out, Abdollah eventually realized that Muhammad's revelations could not have been divine if he could have such liberty to change them; and so he left Muhammad, renounced Islam, and moved to Mecca."

"How did Muhammad respond to that?"

"Well, when he conquered Mecca, Abdollah was one of the first people he killed."

"I guess Muhammad's pride had to be avenged," I commented.

"More than that," my mother-in-law said emphatically. "Abdollah's convincing conclusions, that he openly shared, were a direct challenge to Muhammad's claim that his Sura's were perfect in every respect because they were written by Allah himself in heaven."

"That's interesting," I noted. "So, any changes to the Suras would be an unacceptable notion to the Muslims."

"Yes, it would have been and still is, but the fact is, there were many more changes to come."

"Really? How?"

"Well you see, after the death of Muhammad, his Suras were gathered which had been written on palm leaves, tree bark, stones, and bones, and such like as he had dictated, and a Caliph, or Muslim leader by the name of Uthman came along later and assumed the laborious job of putting them together and creating what we know today as the Qur'an. The Shiite Muslims claim that Uthman left out twenty-five percent of the original verses for political reasons.

The example is used that one Sura, before Uthman standardized the text, was comprised of two hundred verses which now contains only seventy-three."

"Surely the Muslims cannot claim perfection for the Qur'an in the light of that knowledge."

"Oh, but they do. It is an impregnable dogma. They claim unmovable perfection for the Qur'an. Even the language of the Qur'an is claimed to be written in perfect Arabic."

"That seems to be a point that could easily be refuted."

"It is," my mother-in-law said with dismay. "The fact is, the Qur'an contains many grammatical errors and is concluded by many scholars to be a very poorly written document!"

"Wow," I said while shaking my head. "The whole thing seems such an incredible imposition on the thinking and reasoning of any intelligent person."

"It is like any cult, Sarah," my mother-in-law said gently. "Its followers fail to investigate its claims and its leaders refuse to acknowledge its invalidity."

"And," I concluded, " 'My people are destroyed for lack of knowledge,' just like the Bible says."

"Yes," my mother-in-law answered sorrowfully. "Just like the Bible says."

I was struck suddenly by the sadness in my mother-in-law's eyes. The burden she carried for her people was sincere and heavy. A feeling that I had seen these eyes with this same burden overwhelmed me. And then I remembered. I had seen them in the face of my beloved. My husband, John, carried this same weight of responsibility and love for the Arab peoples that his mother did, and the same compassion for them eluded from the inheritance of those same dark eyes. But seeing them this time was different for me. I saw them in a new light, with a new understanding. The burden that I saw there was becoming my own.

Fifteen

Later, as we made our way to the mission work, my heart was heavy with the things my mother-in-law and I had discussed earlier. With every passing car and every Arab who passed us on foot, I would grieve. I would grieve for their lost soul and the victory Satan had won over them through his deception. How loyal they were to this false way. If religion alone and good works could save one, surely their fidelity would win them a place in eternity. Yet, for all their constant bowing toward Mecca and for all their repetitious prayers, even the most consistent of them could not be sure that his good works would outweigh his bad in the end. Like every cult, they believe a great balance or scale will decide their fate. Like every person enveloped in those systems of belief, they are filled with self doubt and fear.

A desire to tell them the good news of the Gospel suddenly arrested me. I wanted to roll down my window and sing to the top of my lungs, "Jesus paid it all, all to Him I owe, sin had left a crimson stain, He washed it white as snow!"

My mother-in-law glanced my way and noticed the tears that were streaming down my face. She tenderly touched my hand then and said knowingly, "God bless you my daughter."

When we reached the mission, my heart was filled with anticipation and joy to see a work being done among these people. A great desire to be a help and encouragement filled me and although I realized that I could not speak their language, I hoped that the love of Christ could be seen and felt through my eyes and arms.

The inner city building was old and weather-beaten without even a sign indicating that there was a church meeting being conducted inside. I wondered how people even knew to come to this place. I asked my mother-in-law.

"The church is advertised by word of mouth," she answered. "The pastor feels that this is the best way to evangelize here."

I doubted this approach, but said nothing. Who was I to question their methods, I thought, but when I walked inside and saw the many vacant seats, my mind began to run with possibilities of how to fill them.

This train of thought was interrupted when the pastor and his wife came to greet me. They were a very pleasant pair and offered a warm welcome. The pastor spoke a little English and told my mother-in-law that he would ask their special speaker to preach slowly so that she could interpret for me. I was humbled by this show of kindness and tried hard to show my appreciation. The pastor said that it was he who was appreciative and honored by my presence and hoped that I would receive a blessing. When he left us to greet the others in attendance, I was left with the feeling that here I had met someone who was indeed filled with the presence of God.

When the service began, and we stood to sing "Amazing Grace" in Arabic, my heart began to swell and again, tears coursed down my cheeks. For though the language was different, the tune remained the same and to see these people sing of the grace of God in a place where this grace was not understood by most, was a tremendous blessing to my heart.

My mother-in-law and I sat at the back of the room, apart from the others so that she could interpret for me. I had never before wished to know a language so badly as I did that evening. My mother-in-law was doing a good job, however, and when the preaching began, I found myself hanging on to her every word.

"God loves Arabs," was the preacher's opening comment. "His desire to draw them to Himself has never changed since Arab generations took shape. These families were from the beginning sought of the Lord and throughout the Bible we can see that God used many of them in a mighty way to accomplish His will. Among these patriots we can find Caleb, whose name means 'conqueror' in Arabic and was descended from people usually associated with Arabs. Caleb had an unmovable trust in the power of God, and God blessed him because, as the scripture says, '. . . he had another spirit with him and hath followed me fully. . . .'

"Another noteworthy Arab in scripture is the widow of Zarephath, whom God used to sustain the prophet Elijah in a time of famine. Furthermore, it is possible that some or all of the wise men who came from the east to worship the Messiah, the Lord Jesus and bring Him gifts, were Arabs.

"You see, my beloved," the preacher continued, "Arabs have a great potential for faith and devotion toward their Creator. It can be seen all around us through their misguided attempt to worship the god of Muhammad whom they have been taught by tradition to obey and serve. But hear me now, my people, Allah is no god! He is the invention of a man, who although may have been sincere, nevertheless produced this god within his own imagination and perhaps, with the aid of the dark kingdom. And do not be deceived by those who would have you believe that the God of the Bible and Allah are one in the same. They are as opposed in character and purpose as mercy is from indifference.

"Muhammad, like many a cult leader, took some of the precious truths of creation and the Creator and dissolved them into the mixing bowl of his creation. A product so arranged that any religious seeker could reach in and find something to pacify that longing in his heart to know the truth. But it is a deception, and even to those who name the name of Christ is this deception reached and the poison of compromise has seeped through the cracks of tolerance until even some of the elect feel threatened by the confusing and insidious religious jargon. But stand to it now!" the preacher declared. "Be clear in your focus and true to your faith in God! Know the Scripture and be aware of the devices of Satan. The misguided effort to blend the Qur'an and the Bible can only serve in causing a man or woman to miss the person of God altogether, and blind their eyes to the love He has offered through His Son.

"You see," the preacher continued, "law is the foundation of Islam. Muslims have no concept of a loving, gracious Father that the true and living God really is. Allah would never stoop to offer his love and heart so freely to mankind, only to receive their rejection and disbelief. Allah demands, not gives. He only will punish those who will not bow to him daily, and perform his commands. He offers no mercy.

" 'But God,' the true and living God that the Bible declares!" the preacher shouted, "'who is rich in mercy, for his great love wherewith he loved us. Even when we were dead in sins, hath quickened us together with Christ, (by grace ye are saved;) And hath raised us up together and made us sit together in heavenly places in Christ Jesus: That in the ages to come he might shew the exceeding riches of his grace in his kindness toward us through Christ Jesus. For by grace are ye saved through faith; and that not of yourselves: it is the gift of God: Not of works, lest any man should boast' (Ephesians 2:4–9)."

The preacher continued to expound on the love and mercy and grace of God; and with each verse he quoted my heart would burst with thankfulness and joy. At one point, he began to sing. It was a familiar song and before I knew it, I was singing it with him, softly in English, though he sang in Arabic. We sang, "Marvelous grace of our loving Lord, freely bestowed on all who believe, you who are longing to see His face, will you this moment His grace receive? Grace, grace, God's grace, grace that is greater than all our sin. Grace, grace, God's grace, grace that is greater than all our sin."

When the song ended I was crying profusely. I looked over at my mother-in-law and she was crying too. She grabbed my hand and squeezed it.

The preacher was bringing the message to a close and offering the people who sat in the room with us who had not received the grace of God through the blood of the Lord Jesus, to come forward and accept His offer of salvation and redemption. I bowed my head and prayed for those to come to Christ.

"The Bible says," the preacher declared, " 'But God commendeth his love toward us, in that, while we were yet sinners, Christ died for us,' Romans 5:8. It says in Romans 6:23, 'For the wages of sin is death: but the gift of God is eternal life through Jesus Christ our Lord.' And then we have this promise later in that same book in chapter 10:9–13, which says, 'That if thou shalt confess with thy mouth the Lord Jesus, and shalt believe in thine heart that God hath raised him from the dead, thou shalt be saved. For with the heart man believeth unto righteousness; and with the mouth confession is made unto salvation. For the scripture saith, Whosoever believeth on him shall not be ashamed. For there is no difference between the Jew and the Greek: for the same Lord over all is rich unto all that call upon him. For whosoever shall call upon the name of the Lord shall be saved.' "

With the invitation given, the preacher stepped in front of the pulpit to receive and help those who would come to accept Christ. A few did respond and it thrilled my heart.

After the service, my mother-in-law thanked the special speaker for his message while I stood beside her nodding my head in agreement. She spoke then to the pastor for a moment, and afterwards, we walked outside and made our way to the car.

"That was a wonderful message!" I exclaimed as we drove away. "One that every Muslim should hear!"

"Yes, the preacher was very brave," my mother-in-law spoke soberly. "Not very often have I heard the Word here preached with such boldness. It is usually softened so not to offend, which results many times in causing the hearer to miss the crucial elements of the message."

"Why, it must be preached boldly!" I declared with passion. "What's the point if it is not!"

My mother-in-law smiled at me and patted my hand. "You have the heart of an evangelist, my daughter. Use it wisely."

"We need to get more people to the service tomorrow night," I said.

"As a matter of fact," my mother-in-law answered, "I'll be coming early to town tomorrow to pick up some refreshments for after the service tomorrow night. Pastor thought it might be an incentive for our people to bring visitors to the meeting. Arabs love cakes and sweets, especially if it's free!"

"Doesn't everyone," I answered smiling.

After arriving home and after my mother-in-law had gone to bed, I slipped outside behind her tent and walked a little ways into the desert to be alone and pray. My heart was still heavy for the Arab peoples and with all that I had witnessed earlier. I knew there was something that I had to get settled.

At first, as I gazed into the star-lit sky, I could not think of a thing to say to my Lord. All I felt was shame. Shame for the selfish life I had led and shame that I had placed my selfish goals above any desire that God might have had for my life. For so long I had pushed the gentle nudging of the Holy Spirit aside and embraced instead a worldly ambition that seemed now so foolish and vain. For what had I given my life? For a few trophies that sat on a dusty shelf. For the praise of Walt, or even my colleagues, who had not even the foggiest notion of what this life is really about?

And what was worse, not only did I place vain ambition before my Lord, I gave a man of flesh and blood, my husband John, that position in my heart that should only belong to God. For John, I had moved aside my career to second place, consigning the Lord of all to a pitiful third.

All of my life I had been taught that God desires and deserves to have first place in our lives. It is demonstrated in the giving to Him of the first of our increase—our tithe. It is shown in our yielding to Him the first day of the week in which to worship His name. How could I have known this principle in my mind and yet failed to accomplish it in my heart? Yes, I paid my tithe. Yes, I always went to church on Sunday, but somehow, I missed the point.

My thoughts went then to the young pastor and wife who labored here so courageously for the Lord. I could see them at the throne of God, when they receive their eternal reward. How joyful they will be to lay down before the Lord Jesus their rewards for the life they have lived and the souls that they have brought to Him.

And what will I say when my name is called? To present to the One who paid my sin's debt, a life lived only for vain adulations could only prove to bring shame and regret.

And then I asked the Lord out loud, "But Father, perhaps you wish for me to be a witness for you in this realm of investigative reporting?" But as soon as the question came forth from my lips, I knew the answer. Perhaps for some God would use this way, but it was not for me. For with my heart God had long been dealing. Even as a child I had known this tugging at my heart to do something special with my life for God. Constantly I had pushed that still small voice away and constantly I had reassured myself that surely God would be pleased with my worldly successes. But it would do no more, for God had this night crystallized what my life consisted of, what my future would hold, and what was His perfect will for me.

Trembling, I knelt on my knees and looked toward the heavens. It was no small thing to surrender my will for His. Not that I didn't want to, but the realization that it was so long in coming broke my heart and I could not speak. At last a cry came forth and with it a plea for forgiveness. And that still night, I laid it all at the feet of my Lord, all my dreams, all my aspirations, all of my love, and all of my life.

It was a night of full surrender and a night so abundant with the presence of God, that it would forever be imprinted in my heart. For He came and comforted me so profoundly as I had never known before. It was a revelation to realize such joy in pleasing Him, and I knew that it would be the focus of my life to find that place again and again for as long as I would live.

It was to the Arab peoples that He would have me sent. I knew assuredly that night that it was His desire to reach out to them and show them His love through His sacrifice, by my witness. How He would accomplish this with the threads of my marriage dangling in the wind, I wasn't sure, but I realized that it was my responsibility only to yield and His to make a way. My course was set then, my purpose was clear. God had called and I had surrendered to be a missionary to the Arab peoples. I would never look back.

Sixteen

he next morning I woke with a peace and a joy that astounded me. I picked up my Bible and read, and with each verse the Holy Spirit came and confirmed the reading within my soul. His leading was so clear and the words jumped out at me as God seemed to spoon-feed me as never before. It was wonderful to receive such individual attention from the Lord, and I marveled at what riches a surrendered heart and life had brought. No more would I be driven by ambition, but the success I would, henceforth, value in life would be to dwell in the presence of God and to know this peace, fresh every morning.

I went through that morning and afternoon with a song in my heart and a feeling of exuberance that I couldn't contain. My heart was clean and my conscience was clear! At last, the thing that hindered my spiritual life was swept away and in its place I found a joy that was wonderful! I wondered at the pride that kept me back for so long and its deception that my happiness would be lost in surrender. What a lie! I had never known such joy and contentment.

At last, the time came for my mother-in-law and me to go into town to buy refreshments for the revival that night. All the way there, I talked about the meeting the previous evening and the need to bring the lost to the service to come. My mother-in-law chuckled at my excitement and said she wished she could have me around all the time to motivate her for the work of God. I told her my news then, of my previous night's surrender and with that she stopped and pulled the car off to the side of the road. She turned then with serious eyes and put her arms around my neck. At length, we were both crying and rejoicing in what the future might bring.

By the time we arrived at the bakery, which was across the street from where the church met, I was full of reckless vision! How I wanted to fill the church house that night with the lost! I thought of passing out invitations on the street and even considered making a sign to wear on my back. And then I had what I thought was a brilliant idea.

My mother-in-law was buying little cakes then for that evening and I asked her how many she was getting.

"Oh, I thought fifty would be enough," she answered.

"Fifty!" I said aghast. "That room can hold at least a hundred and fifty!"

"We'll never have that many, Sarah. The food will just go to waste."

"Buy two hundred, mother," I said with confidence. "I'll pay for it."

My mother-in-law smiled at me and shook her head.

"Just indulge me," I said putting my arm around her shoulder.

"All right," she said reluctantly. "I guess we can serve them throughout the week."

"Great!" I said as I turned to leave.

"Where are you going?" my mother-in-law asked.

"Don't worry," I answered. "I'll be back."

"Be careful."

I found a small print shop around the corner and proceeded to work out my idea. Thankfully, the Arab man behind the counter could speak a little English. I told him that I wanted fifty posters that said, "All Muslims invited for free cakes and refreshments. Hear fellow Arab speak an important message!" I included the time and address and asked that he print them in Arabic. I simply had to trust that he would write what I asked him to.

With the posters in hand, I proceeded to tack them on

every light post and vacant building that I could find. At last, they all were distributed and I made my way back to the meeting place with a satisfied smile playing on my lips.

"Where have you been?" my mother-in-law asked when I arrived.

I smiled. "It's a secret," I said.

The food was placed on long tables in an adjoining room. My mother-in-law had not put out all that we had bought and so I did this myself without her knowledge. "Oh ye of little faith," I chuckled to myself as I did so.

When the service was drawing near, people began to pour into the building. I looked at my mother-in-law with glee and on her face she wore a look of astonishment. The pastor stood nearby, and I turned to see his reaction. To my surprise, he looked more concerned than anything else. This puzzled me.

Soon, every chair was filled and the pastor went nervously to the platform to begin the service. After a welcome was given, he proceeded to lead the assembly in a congregational song. The song we sang was entitled "Oh, How I Love Jesus," and only a few present knew the words. The rest of the crowd looked around at each other in disturbed silence and I wondered at this. After that, a couple went forward to sing a duet. I did not recognize the song, but I did sense an amount of resentment from the crowd as they sang. Things were not going well.

At this juncture a man walked in who was somehow familiar. Then I remembered. It was the man who had picked me up in the desert and carried me to the encampment of my mother-in-law on a camel. He still wore those dirty fatigues. My mother-in-law saw him too and a look of concern spread across her face. Then he turned and looked at the two of us standing there. His face showed his surprise before he turned and sat down in the back row.

I looked at my mother-in-law then and asked, "Isn't that . . ."

"Yes," she whispered before I had finished the question. "He is my kin."

The worried look on her face said it all and I wondered what I had done.

At last, the guest speaker rose to address the crowd. I prayed that all would go well and that the gospel would be clearly given.

The preacher opened the sermon with First John 5:12 and read plainly, "He that hath the Son hath life: and he that hath not the Son of God hath not life." With this verse read, a murmuring began to spread throughout the room. As the speaker preached on about the salvation God offered through His Son, the Lord Jesus, the murmuring grew louder. Then suddenly a man leaped to his feet and shouted in Arabic, "*La ilaha illa lah, wa muhammadu rasul ilahi!*" which in English is, "There is no god but Allah and Muhammad is the apostle of god!"

It was a signal for an uproar, as another and another stood to shout the words over and over in repetitious chorus. With each cry, the voices built in intensity until most all of the crowd had erupted into a reverberating chant. Then chairs began to smash and men leaped to stand on them while clenching their fists, as the peaceful gathering had turned into a dangerous demonstration.

My mother-in-law grabbed my arm and as our eyes met I realized the gravity of the situation. And then suddenly the pastor was shouting and somehow his voice carried above the din.

"Wait," he yelled. "There is food! We will eat now!"

With that said, he went and took the first man he could by the arm and led him to where the food was laid out. Amazingly, the shouting subsided and a line formed through the doorway. I couldn't believe it.

Before I could comment on the turn of the crowd, my mother-in-law grabbed me by the hand and led me outside and to the car. We raced away and didn't speak until we were out of the city. My mother-in-law pulled off the side of the road then and put her head on the steering wheel.

"Sarah," she said slowly after a moment. "Did you have something to do with bringing that crowd in?"

"Well . . ." I muttered, feeling guilty.

My mother-in-law looked me squarely in the eye.

"Well, I guess I did," I admitted finally. "I made posters inviting Muslims and advertising free food and put them around the city."

My mother-in-law let out a long sigh.

"I didn't know it would turn out like that. I only wanted to reach the Muslims for Christ."

My mother-in-law put her hand on mine. "I don't doubt your motives, my darling, but why did you not seek counsel before you acted?"

I said nothing but thought, if she knew me better, she would know that that was the story of my life. Never do I think before I act!

"You see, we never allow ourselves to be out-numbered. It is by design that we do not advertise, but rather seek to reach the lost one by one."

"I understand now."

"Someone could have been hurt," my mother-in-law said soberly. "The work here in Basra may be closed by the government."

I sunk low in my seat.

My mother-in-law started the car again then and said, "I hope the pastor and his wife and the speaker and our people got out all right."

We drove home in silence. I was miserable and berated myself all the way home. Why didn't I ask my mother-in-law or the pastor, or better yet, why didn't I inquire of the Lord before I went on in my hasty mission? Must I always rush into things? This time it was not only myself that I put at risk, but men and women of God, and a fledgling church! The folly was my own. I could not deny it.

When we arrived home the situation grew worse, for as soon as we entered my mother-in-law's tent, her brother, the sheik, came bounding in after us. His face was contorted with anger and he began shouting immediately at my mother-in-law in Arabic.

He was so angry that I thought he would hit her and then suddenly he turned to me. To my surprise, he was shouting in English.

"And you! An American!" he spat. "It was you who brought my sister to this treasonous religious meeting!"

"No!" my mother-in-law said loudly and came to stand between myself and her enraged brother.

He pushed her out of the way, knocking her to the floor.

"You bring shame into my tribe," he said to me again. "Just when we are about to make history!"

"Make history?" I asked trembling.

"Do you not know?" he asked in disbelief. "We are at war with your government!"

"You are?!"

"We," he said proudly, "are the San'ie!"

My mouth dropped open with that declaration and I thought I would faint. Instead, I felt the sheik's powerful grip on my arm as he drug me outside.

"You see?" he said, as he stopped and pointed toward the east. "You see that smoke in the distance? There we have your people and there they will be murdered unless your government delivers the military advancements that we have demanded! And they will deliver! We shall be victorious!"

My knees wobbled beneath me and I felt like a rag doll, standing only by the strength of his crushing grip.

"We shall march on from there across the face of the whole world," he raged on, "and conquer all of civilization for Islam in the ultimate holy war!"

I was speechless with shock as I looked at the madman in horror.

"But you!" he said to me then in disgust. "You have brought dishonor to my family through my sister."

"What are you going to do with me?" I asked trembling.

"If you see the next sunset," he said with hatred, "it will be a disgrace to Allah!"

Seventeen

I was taken to the sheik's tent and again placed in the women's quarters. The ladies there looked at me warily and some with pity, but none came near. I was left alone in a dark corner to await my fate.

I had never known such fear in all of my life and the anxiety it caused robbed me of a clear mind. Unanswered questions crowded my thoughts as I wondered why my mother-in-law had not told me who it was I was staying among and warn me of the danger it presented. And what was I doing here anyway? I came to find my husband in the guise of writing a story. Neither had I pursued and it seemed I never would.

My thoughts went round and around in this vein until the wee hours of the morning while all slept around me oblivious of my torment. And then the thought came to me. Did I not see my dear husband in the prison camp by satellite? It seemed so like him. Must I die only a short distance from where he is imprisoned, never reassuring him of my love? Could I make it there somehow? What did I have to lose anyway!

Without another consideration I sat up from where I lay. I would slide underneath the side of the tent and go to my husband. Not only did I have the chance of seeing him once more, there was also the possibly of rescue along with the other hostages from the U.S.— a possibility that wasn't afforded me if I stayed here. I had to at least try.

As quietly as I could, I crawled over to the tent wall. It was tightly fastened down and only slightly was I able to lift it, but it was enough! With my face pressed in the sand, I wormed my way underneath the heavy goats' hair fabric. I was out!

Spitting sand, I stood to my feet and looked toward the east, where the dawn was just beginning to lighten the sky. The trail of smoke marked my destination and to it I began to run. Fueled by adrenaline and fear, I ran through the heavy sand on the wings of desperation. Before it seemed humanly possible, the old prison camp emerged on the horizon like a mirage.

It was an ancient building, made of concrete and barbed wire. There were trash cans lined up against the wall, all painted like American flags. An Arabian soldier sat dozing at the entrance with his machine gun leaning on his chest.

As I walked slowly up to the compound, I wondered if I could take him by surprise and appropriate his gun. That fantasy was shortlived, for he quickly was aroused by my footsteps and stood suddenly with an expression of surprise on his face.

He said something to me in Arabic and then grabbed me by the arm. I did not resist as he thrust me inside the prison doors and down a number of concrete steps. We entered a musty room that was lined with barred prison cells. Inside the cells, I saw the women hostages huddled against the walls in an effort to keep warm. The soldier took a key from his pocket, and with a yawn, he opened one of the cells and shoved me inside. He said something again in Arabic and then turned and walked back up the steps.

The women in the next cells came and stood with astonishment before their bars and stared at me.

"Who are you?" one of them asked. "The guard thought you were one of us who escaped!"

"I'm a reporter with the *Seattle Times*," I answered.

"You mean the army can't get to us, but the news can!" another said sarcastically.

129

They all stared at me in disbelief.

"Well, actually it's a long story," I said and proceeded to explain. ". . . So you see," I said when I had finished, "I'm here, most of all, to try and see my husband if I possibly can."

"You really think you saw him by satellite?" one of the women asked. "That's wild."

"I'd never do what you did for any man!" another commented.

"You don't know my husband," I answered.

"And you really think he's one of the hostages?"

"I'm not sure," I said looking down at my feet.

"Well, one thing is for sure," the woman said emphatically. "You're one of the hostages now!"

I looked at the four women then, and thought, What a stupid fool they must think I am. And they're right! I put my hands over my weary face then and lowered my head.

"Don't worry," one of the women said kindly. "I have great faith in our military. They'll get us out."

"She has every right to worry!" another said abruptly. "We all may die before the week is out!"

The kindly woman looked at her sharply and then back at me. "I'm afraid she's getting a little hysterical," she whispered.

I turned then and looked around the room that we were in. "Where are the men kept?" I asked.

"They are somewhere upstairs. We see them occasionally when we are taken to the prison yard to get some air."

"If you can call that stifling desert wind—air!" one of them said wryly.

"Do you think there's any way that the Arab guerrillas will let me speak to my husband?" I asked.

"You can ask the captain of the guards when he inspects in about an hour. But I don't envy you that!"

"Why?"

"He's a very harsh and brutal man. I've seen the Marines after he has beaten them. They can hardly walk."

"Oh no!"

"Yes, and our men that are hostages are no wimps, but I've never seen men that were so afraid of another as they are of the captain!"

I swallowed hard and thought of my John. I could not imagine him being afraid of another man. This captain must be inhuman.

I sat in my cell then, awaiting the time of inspection. It would be ridiculous for me to even consider asking this man for anything, I thought. He probably would have no mercy for me anyway when he learns who I am from the sheik. I turned my face to the wall then in shame and fear. All I could do was pray.

Finally, the time came when we were all ordered out of our cells. The other women and I lined up for the notorious captain to inspect us. I was trembling badly and my knees knocked together uncontrollably. The captain marched along in front of the other women, yelling at them in Arabic.

My eyes were downcast as he came and stood before me. I looked up slowly, with trepidation, and then stared at him in astonishment. It was John!

Obviously, he was as amazed to see me as I was to see him. My mouth began to form his name, but before I could speak, he shouted something in Arabic and shoved us back into our cells.

I stood in my cell, staring out into the corridor in complete confusion. My John . . . a guerrilla? It couldn't be! This was almost too much for me to comprehend. Did he go back to his people after our fight? Surely he wouldn't throw off all he knew and turn from his God!

After about an hour, my mind was still whirling with questions when I heard the jingle of keys. John was opening the barred door of my cell.

"Sarah," he whispered loudly. "Come with me."

"John!" I said happily, and then turned to wake up the other women who had laid down and gone to sleep.

"No!" he said sharply. "Just you!"

He helped me out of the cell, up the stairs, and outside to where an empty jeep sat waiting with the keys dangling in the ignition.

"Take the jeep," he said quietly. "Drive it about ten miles south to a red brick two-story house. It will have a large old barn next to it with a picture of the Ayatollah Khomeini painted on the entire south wall."

"John," I said facing him. "I'm not going anywhere until you tell me what you're doing in this horrible place and dressed in this madman's uniform!"

"Sarah," he said angrily, "I've risked everything to get you this jeep. Now get in and go!"

"No!" I screamed. "Those women said you were a cruel and brutal man . . . what's happened to you? You're a traitor, aren't you!"

John's face flushed red. He gritted his teeth and yelled, "Get in the jeep!"

I got in the jeep. I turned the key and drove off in the direction he had said, without looking back.

Eighteen

Tears blinded my eyes, as I drove south into the desert. There was no fear left in my heart. No worry about where I was going or concern for the future. I didn't care if I died in this dry and arid wasteland. My mind was numb with confusion and my body was limp from exhaustion. The adrenaline that had kept me going had ceased and I wanted nothing more than to stop the jeep and let myself sob.

But I kept going. Soon the red brick house and barn came into view and I pulled up next to them. I didn't know what John had wanted me to do. Perhaps he intended to meet me here. Yes, that was it. I would go inside the house and wait.

I was encouraged with the thought of seeing John. For whatever he had become, I knew that I still loved him. Whether or not that made sense, the fact remained. He was in my heart and I still needed desperately to tell him so.

But what if he has changed, I questioned then. What if there are aspects to his nature that were never revealed outside of this alien environment. I had read several cases of young women who had married Arab men and moved to their homelands, only to find that once there, their husbands became entirely different men when placed among their national customs and prejudices. Would I still love him if that were the case? It was a deflating thought and I tried to shove it aside.

I got out of the jeep then and proceeded to make my way to the house. It was so quiet that it seemed eerie and I wondered if anyone occupied the dilapidated farm. Realizing that I could easily spook myself, I did my best to remain calm. But then I heard something. It was footsteps. My heart began to beat wildly and I froze in my place, unable to move.

And then a man emerged from around the side of the house. It was an American soldier, and I thought I would die with relief.

"You there," he said coming toward me.

I stared after him as he came and stood before me.

"You're that reporter that has been missing, aren't you," he stated rather than asked.

"Yes," I said wearily. "I'm Sarah Morgan."

"We've been looking high and low for you."

"I'm sorry."

"You'd better come with me," he said with authority.

"But I . . . I want to wait here."

"Are you crazy?" he said and took me by the elbow. "You're coming with me."

I let him lead me away and over to the jeep that I had come in.

"We'll take this," he said opening the door for me.

He drove the jeep further south until we reached a beachfront. There was a boat hidden behind some boulders and we got inside it and cast off.

I didn't say another word as we sped across the water. My heart was heavy and my mind was overloaded. There were fish jumping carefreely in the water alongside of us, and at these I stared, thankful for an alternate focus.

When we reached the island base, there was a crowd of people waiting on the beach to receive us. Among them were the other reporters and Ivan. They were taking pictures and I turned my head away from them. Ivan came to help me out of the boat.

"There now, sister," he said kindly, as he steadied me on the beach. "You've sure had us worried. "

I let him lead me through the crowd, up the bank, and into the complex without saying a word. The entourage followed behind.

Once inside, I was halted by General Pierce who stood with arms folded and feet apart, waiting for me to enter. I stood before him feeling like a naughty child receiving a silent scolding. For what seemed an eternity, he just looked at me, not saying a word. Then finally he spoke to all the reporters who stood there with their notepads and pens awaiting.

"Now that you are all here," he said with authority, "you are to pack your things and be ready to leave in one hour. Be prompt!" With that, he was gone.

With my mouth open I watched him leave while Ivan whispered, "I think he means business."

Before long we were on a plane, flying east to Jerusalem in the same route we had come. Again, we would catch a bus to Tel Aviv and from there, fly home to the States.

I was flocked on the plane by reporters asking questions and for once I knew how it felt to be hounded by the press. It wasn't a pleasant experience. Finally, Ivan, sensing my discomfort ordered them away.

"Go sit down," he scolded. "Can't you see she's all done in!"

"Thank you, Ivan," I whispered when they had left.

"Don't worry," he said patting my hand. "I'll take care of you, and when you're ready to talk about it, I'm here."

But I didn't say a word the whole trip. I just couldn't. How could I put into words the fears I nursed within about my own husband. Like a whipped puppy, I allowed Ivan to lead me around from the plane to the bus and then off again at Tel Aviv. He was worried about me, I could tell. My spirit was broken and the energy that once defined my personality had evaporated.

"Tell you what," he said, as we stood in the bus terminal at Tel Aviv, "let's go back to that hotel in Jaffa that you liked so much. We have to spend the night somewhere any-way."

I appreciated Ivan's concern and effort to comfort me. At this point, however, it really didn't matter to me where we went. He hailed a cab, nevertheless, and we were on our way.

Soon we arrived in Jaffa and again checked into the nostalgic Casablanca hotel. All I wanted to do this time was go to bed, and so after declining Ivan's offer to buy my dinner, I made my way up to my room. It seemed forever since I had laid my body down on a soft bed and before I knew it, I had drifted off into an exhaustive sleep.

Nineteen

I awoke feeling disoriented. It was dark now and I had no idea what time it was. For a moment I laid there as everything came back to me. How I wished it were all a bad dream that I could forget and dismiss.

The waves from the Mediterranean sent a soothing melody to my ears and I decided to go and sit out on the terrace after I had taken a much needed shower. The hot water pounding on my back felt good and then with the thick terry cloth robe that the hotel provided, wrapped snugly about me, my spirits were almost lifted.

Again, it was a beautiful evening with stars shining and orange blossoms in bloom. Again, as I stood out on that moonlit terrace, I longed to be there with my beloved. My love for John, I realized, was still as strong as ever. Even in the compromise of his integrity, my heart still clung to the memory of his embrace.

I had let the moment pass to assure him of that love. I had my chance and now it was gone. Would he ever know how I felt?

Then suddenly I heard a key slide in the lock of the door to my room. I turned and watched the knob move and the door open—and there he stood. My heart burst with joy.

"John!" I cried in wonder as he came toward me.

I ran to him then and threw myself into his arms.

"Is it really you?" I cried, as my hands traveled over and over his face to make sure he was real.

"It's me, Sarah," he answered huskily.

"I love you, John," I said tearfully, fearing I may lose the chance to tell him again. "I love you so much!"

"Sarah," he said taking my face in his hands, "you love me even though you think I'm a traitor?"

"I love you no matter what you are!"

Then he kissed me. A kiss that would burn in my memory for as long as I would live.

"I came on the fastest plane," he said then with earnest. "I couldn't stand for you to think that I was a traitor."

"Then what?"

"I was a spy, Sarah," he said with eyes pleading for understanding. "I was placed in that situation by the military, because of my family connection to the San'ie."

"But how?"

"For some time," he answered, "our government knew that the San'ie were becoming hostile and sent me over periodically to gain their trust. I won them over with financial help and a convincing assumption of Islam. When they abducted the hostages, I had to fly over immediately and meet them at the prison camp."

"The night of our fight?"

"Yes, that night."

"Why didn't you leave word to me where you were?"

"It all happened so fast. I intended to write you as I flew out on the plane, but the military wouldn't allow it because of your connection to the newspaper. It was top secret."

"Oh . . ."

"It tore me apart, Sarah!" he cried then. "I wished a hundred times that I would have at least left you a note telling you that I loved you and that I would be back. I didn't know that I would not get another chance."

"Oh, John!" I said, while tears rolled down my face. "I wished a hundred times that I had not said those awful words to you that I did! I had to find you to tell you it wasn't true!"

"I knew it wasn't true the minute you spoke," he answered tenderly. "I know you better than that."

"What about your mother?" I asked after a moment. "Did she know about your espionage?"

"Yes, she played along. It was the only way to prevent her family and the hostages from getting hurt. Our military could have wiped the San'ie out in a moment. It was her intervention and mine that saved the lives of our people."

"What happened? How is it that you are here now?"

"Well, as you know the U.S. was trying to negotiate a peaceful settlement. That would have saved any embarrassment for my mother or myself and the San'ie, but they wouldn't have it. Myself and the other Marines that were 'hostages,' had all been planted to take over the situation if a settlement could not be reached. Our mission was called 'Silent Storm' and we had planned to engage the mission at the end of this week. Then you showed up," he said looking at me with exasperation, "and we had to expedite things."

"You mean . . ."

"Yes, it's over. Just a few hours ago, I and my men took over the entire prison camp and confiscated all of their artillery, ammunition, and even a small plane and tank that they were so proud of."

"And the guards, the San'ie?"

"We locked them up in their own cells and took the keys," he said with a chuckle. "My uncle, the sheik, will have a hard time getting his men out!"

"What about the hostages?"

"They are on their way home as we speak."

I let out a sigh of relief. "I put the whole mission in jeopardy then, didn't I?" I asked then with concern.

"I'm afraid so," he answered reluctantly.

"Well, it's their own fault! The military, that is," I said defensively. "They should have told me what was going on!"

"Who would have thought my girl would cross the globe

to find me!" he laughed.

"Oh, John, I'm sorry!"

"Sorry? For loving me that much?" he said as he pulled me closer. "I must be the luckiest man alive!"

I leaned into his embrace.

"They were about to tell you anyway, you know."

"They were?"

"Yes. Apparently, General Pierce had decided it was safer to let you in on things, but before he had the chance to tell you, you disappeared."

I grimaced.

"What about your mother?" I asked then.

"As soon as the operation was over, I went and took her to a safe place. She's staying with her pastor and his wife."

"And they and their people are all okay?"

"So far, so good."

"I'm so relieved!"

"Everything is fine, Sarah," he said stroking my hair.

"So, you didn't beat those Marines then?" I asked.

"Beat them! They were under my command! And pretty good actors, I might add," he said with a smile. "I could have never taken them all on by myself anyway. They were the most highly trained and skilled soldiers that our military had to offer! That's why their names were withheld from the media. We feared if the San'ie learned who they were, they would become suspicious."

"How did they become hostages?"

"They stormed the place just after I arrived in a staged rescue attempt. They allowed me to 'capture' them and we all had to work hard to maintain the illusion while our government tried to reason with my uncle and his men."

"Oh, John," I cried then. "You're no traitor. You're a hero!"

"And you my love," he said with tenderness, "are the lady of my dreams and the woman of my desire."

I looked deep into his eyes then, while my hands traveled across his broad shoulders and up into his curling hair. How sensitive and sweet it was for him to recite from the precious love letter that had kept me going through all of this. It was as if his soul was part of mine and the grief and the hope I felt, was his as well.

"You'll get a medal of honor for what you've done, John. I'm sure of it," I said.

"As a matter of fact, I've already been assured of being decorated by the president when we get home, Sarah. But there's something that means far more to me that I need to talk to you about."

"What is it?"

"I know this is going to be hard for you to hear, especially after all you've been through. But Sarah," he said taking me by the shoulders, "I've been so burdened for the Arab peoples and for my mother's family during the time that I've spent there. It was terrible to have to deceive them like I did, even if it was for their own good; but I want the chance to share with them what is really important in my life—who I really am. My life is bound up in the Lord. I live and breathe to bring honor and glory to Him. It is the thing that brings me joy and makes my life worthwhile . . ."

"But John . . ."

"I know it's hard for you to understand, but I came to the place, just a few days ago, that I knew in my heart that if I could not spend my life ministering to these people and winning them to Christ, I would never be happy. Sarah, what I'm trying to tell you is that I have surrendered my life to preach the gospel to the Arabs!"

"But John, you must understand . . ."

"I do understand, Sarah," he interrupted. "I understand how important your career is to you. But you must understand this, that receiving a medal of honor from the president is all well and good, but receiving the honor of being called of God is so much greater a privilege to me, that it doesn't compare!"

"Will you shut up for a minute and let me talk?" That startled him. I had never said shut up to him before. "John," I said and then laughed.

"What?"

I couldn't stop laughing. Soon, tears were rolling down my face and John was laughing too.

"What is it?" he said finally bringing me in control.

"John," I said and smiled. "God has called me to be a missionary to the Arab peoples as well. I surrendered to do that not knowing if you would ever be beside me in that task."

"When?"

"Just a few days ago. While I was with your mother, the Lord began to burden my heart."

"Oh, Sarah!" he said crushing me within his strong embrace. "Nothing could mean more to me than that God has knit our hearts together for His work. What a brave and fearless missionary's wife you will be!"

"You mean impetuous and foolhardy."

"That, too!"

"Hey!"

"But I wouldn't have you any other way," he said, and kissed my forehead.

I snuggled down contentedly in his arms. I had my love at last close to me. Our hearts were together in purpose for the work of God. All my regrets had dissolved away. All my mistakes were not to haunt me. I may even learn something from them, I thought. Could it get any better than this?

And then I had a thought. I pulled back in excitement and looked at John in the face.

"What is it?" he asked.

"It may be the last thing I ever do for Walt," I said happily. "But have I got an exclusive story to write!"

THE END